THE UNCOOPERATIVE WARRIOR

THE UNCOOPERATIVE WARRIOR

UNSTOPPABLE LIV BEAUFONT™ BOOK 2

SARAH NOFFKE

MICHAEL ANDERLE

DISRUPTIVE IMAGINATION®

LMBPN Publishing
PMB 196, 2540 South Maryland Pkwy
Las Vegas, NV 89109

First US Edition, February 2019
Version 1.01, February 2019

THE UNCOOPERATIVE WARRIOR TEAM

Thanks to the JIT Readers

Jeff Eaton
Crystal Wren
Daniel Weigert
Angel LaVey
Misty Roa
Keith Verret
John Ashmore
Micky Cocker
Larry Omans
Kelly O'Donnell

If I've missed anyone, please let me know!

Editor
The Skyhunter Editing Team

For Kathy.
Thank you for giving me my first fantasy book.
Since then, the world has been a better place.

CHAPTER ONE

The sound of monks chanting in the distance reminded Adler where he was. It shouldn't have been hard to remember, given the stone walls and ever-present musty smell in the hall, but he still felt disoriented each time he visited this location. *Those were the wards,* he reminded himself. The protections that had been placed on the monastery centuries before to guard that which it held.

Beside him the old monk hurried, the keys in his fingers clattering as he staggered forward, a lantern in his other hand. In the distance, a dripping sound made a pleasant drumming that accompanied the chanting.

"I don't remember the last time I saw you," the monk named Niall said, squinting into the dark.

"You wouldn't," Adler replied, careful to keep the bundle under his robes safe and unseen. The old monk's memory had been wiped so many times that he was close to dementia. Still, in the recesses of the old man's mind, he remembered Adler well enough to let him into the monastery each time. Niall alone knew the path they took through the catacombs under the ancient monastery. When he was close to passing, his knowledge would be passed onto another monk, as it had for centuries.

Adler had never liked entrusting something so important to a mortal, yet that was the safest way. The information wasn't even safe in *his* mind, he believed. Some things were so important that the measures it took to protect them were worth these risks. He rested his hand on the canister under his robe. Stored magic was one of those things. In the wrong hands, it could be earth-shattering. What Adler feared most was that the magic he held now would open doors that had been shut long ago. It was better for everyone this way.

Bats dove from the arched ceiling as the two men strode through the next tunnel. A larger dark form streaked after the bats, startling Niall.

"What was that?" he asked, halting and holding up the lantern.

Adler urged him forward. "It was nothing. Only a shadow."

The old monk didn't look convinced as he inched forward, having to nearly be pushed to continue.

"I'm not sure what it is you do down here," Niall stated. "There's nothing here but endless hallways and entrances to the great spire."

"It is none of your concern." Adler grew restless with worry the longer they stayed down there. The monastery was protected from portal magic, which meant he was trapped if something happened. Not being able to use magic here was part of the protections, although the irony wasn't lost on the old magician.

Niall halted abruptly, a shiver running over his ancient form. He pointed with the lantern. "The location you seek is just ahead."

Alder nodded, striding past the slight man.

"S-s-sir," Niall stuttered, his jaw suddenly chattering as if the chill in the air had frozen him to the core.

Adler spun around, impatience on his face. "Yes?"

"What is it that you keep down there?" The monk scratched his head, thinking hard. "For the life of me, I can't seem to remember, although I know the way. Why is that?"

Adler let out a long breath. He should dismiss the old monk; there wasn't time for chatter. However, Adler knew how the spell worked. It was sealed by the words he'd speak next. "You are the guide, and only to lead one of the Seven to this spot. It protects that which is most sacred, and it cannot be found by anyone but you."

Niall's eyes glazed over for a moment as if he'd suddenly fallen into a trance. Then he shook his head. "Yes, I remember now." He waved his hand, the long, rusty keys clattering with the movement. "Please take your time. I'll be here when you're done."

Adler spun around, not entirely sure where he was going. The hallway split up ahead. He halted at the intersection, where a round blue and green stone on the floor caught his attention. Turning back to where the monk stood, Adler squinted into the dark. Due to the lantern light, he could tell that Niall was resting against a nearby wall with his eyes closed.

Turning his attention back to the stone, Adler read the language that few knew that was inscribed under his feet.

The words rolled off his tongue like the rush of water over rocks, soft and melodic.

Look toward the heavens. Climb high to reach the treasure.

Adler brought his gaze up, realizing at once that the great spire soared overhead, creating an abyss of black. On the walls closest to him, he spied small indentations on the stones—the path one would take if they dared climb to the top. Round and round, all the way to the locked vault at the highest peak of the monastery.

How many times had Adler looked up at this spire, feeling as though he was seeing it for the first time? He didn't know. The wards of protection prevented him from remembering, and yet he knew what was held in the vault, even if he could never remember how to get there.

He withdrew the canister from inside his robe, the light blue substance inside glowing faintly in the mostly dark corridor. Magic never faded, but when not used, it did dull a bit—just like people and creatures.

For Adler, that didn't explain why Olivia Beaufont's magic was so strong after being unlocked. There was much about the girl that perplexed him. He still believed that she was the right choice for Warrior, although he hadn't foreseen her nearly ruining everything. Instead of taking out the Zonks, she'd intervened, botching a plan that had been in the works for a long time.

Adler regarded the canister in his hands with great appreciation and sighed. He tried to remember that things had worked out for the best. If not for Olivia's actions, Valentino's double-crossing might not have been exposed until it was too late. Entrusting a rebellious magician to such a mission had been foolish. It was just that there were so few Adler could trust with such a task. Most would ask questions. Most wouldn't understand. They might think that Adler was collecting and storing the magic for himself. They wouldn't understand that he was cleaning up lost bits of magic. Keeping it safe. Going forward, he'd have to be more careful who he trusted for such things. He might just need to do it himself.

Alder raised his hand, and a small dragon the size of a falcon flew down from the shadows to perch on his glove.

Adler regarded Indikos with affection, catching the spark in his green eyes. He pulled a length of thin rope from his pocket and used it to tie the canister of magic to the dragon's back. He realized at once that he must have done this many times since the act came so naturally, like riding a bike or playing the piano.

Indikos stayed still as the canister was tied into place. After Adler ensured it was tight enough, he lifted his arm into the air and the dragon soared upward, flapping his orange wings until he was swallowed by the darkness. When he returned, the canister of magic would be gone, kept out of the hands of those who must never hold it ever again.

CHAPTER TWO

Liv Beaufont crossed her arms over her chest, looking down at the chaos below her. On the jungle floor, a dozen or more goblins fought over piles of jewelry, electronics, clothes, handbags and other things they'd stolen from the tourists in Bali, Indonesia.

Tracking the little monsters hadn't been hard since they had yelped and snorted as they'd scurried through the jungle. Liv slapped her arm as a mosquito landed, about to bite her.

The damn bugs had been the problem, she thought bitterly. Oh, and the monkeys who kept following her, making it harder for her to stay unseen.

The goblins weren't paying attention to her now, too busy biting and kicking and thrashing each other to get the best prizes.

Liv slid the hood onto her head, keeping her eyes low. She could have stopped the thieves a time or two as she watched them steal and disappear through different resorts.

However, these two-foot-tall green creatures weren't the ones she needed to stop. It was their master who was the problem.

From the largest hut in the camp, a goblin, bigger and uglier than the rest, exited. Trock wore entirely too few clothes and would have benefited from a large mask to cover his pock-marked face. From his long ears, rows of silver rings hung, and on his back was a short sword, its tip still covered in fresh blood. As he progressed closer to the mayhem, the other goblins began to shout more wildly.

Looking down at the feline who stood next to her, Liv pursed her lips. "This would be a perfect chance to throw some fireballs."

"Next time you'll have to have the gnomes teach you how to create them," Plato said, sitting casually on the thatched roof they occupied and looking down at the goblins. "It *is* gnome magic, after all."

Liv agreed with a nod. "Yes, that would have been good to know before I pissed off a slew of them and sullied my name with the lot of them. Now they won't give me a minute to apologize."

Plato lifted his pink nose in the air. "You don't need the gnomes."

"Well, I'd like to know how to make fireballs, so I think I do," Liv stated. "And we all need each other. We are supposed to be sharing this planet."

Plato's green eyes swiveled to the goblin fights. A larger goblin had pulled a stolen laptop away from a smaller one and bonked him on the head with it. The assault cracked the machine, making the first goblin shriek with frustration. "I think the creatures below need a refresher course on how sharing works."

Liv sighed heavily. "Yes, and also to be taught that stealing is wrong." She lifted both her hands and the trees began to rustle like a great storm was about to rip through the island. Dirt and leaves flew up from the ground, covering many of the thrashing creatures. Palm trees bent almost double, looking dangerously close to toppling.

Liv might not have the ability to create fire, but she could harness elements that already existed—in this case, wind. When the camp below was in complete chaos, goblins diving and covering their misshapen faces to escape the debris and others holding onto large plants to anchor themselves to the ground, Liv sprang off the roof of the hut.

She landed in the middle of the clearing, her head down and one hand barely grazing the ground.

The wind stopped at once.

The whimpering of the goblins faded as they realized the wind that had been trying to pull them from the ground was gone. It was replaced by silence as they turned to find the Warrior rising to a standing position in the middle of the open area.

"Magician! How dare you enter our camp?" the chief goblin yelled, charging toward Liv, his head nearly even with her waist. Despite his stature, his jagged teeth and stocky build meant he was a force to be reckoned with. That was why Liv raised her hand at once. A set of ropes on the ground by a nearby tree rose and flew through the air, wrapping around the goblin and tying him into a neat little bundle. He fell over on his side, looking like a candy

SARAH NOFFKE & MICHAEL ANDERLE

bar with his head poking out of one end of the wrapper and his gnarly feet out the other.

"I agree," Liv began, turning in a circle as the other goblins unsheathed their weapons and bared their yellow teeth at her. "The agreement with the House of Seven states that magicians aren't to enter your territory without your permission. But it also says that you aren't to pillage from mortals, does it not?"

The chief had rolled over so that half his mouth was in the dirt. He started making garbled, unintelligible noises.

Liv rolled her eyes, keeping her awareness on the other goblins that were inching closer. She flicked her wrist and the closest one went flying, knocking into a tree trunk. It slid down to the ground with a loud squeak. "Oops. Sorry. Meant to throw you in the pond over there," she said, indicating a disgusting pit of swamp water—a breeding ground for mosquitoes.

A goblin at Liv's back raced toward her and she spun around and held out her hand, lifting the goblin into the air. When he was hovering at her eye level, she clicked her tongue. "Now, I'd rethink this whole attacking idea because I'm still working on this aiming thing. It's going to take some practice."

The goblin kicked his feet angrily, holding a giant fork over his head and calling her names, or at least that was what it sounded like.

She shrugged and sent him toward the pond, but he landed next to a neighboring tree. "See, I told you. I was never good at sports. I throw like an elf." Liv laughed at her own joke. "Get it? Because they are so lanky and all. Their arms get tangled up if they try to pitch a ball."

She continued to laugh. The goblins regarded her with contempt.

"Okay, fine," Liv said, her laughter fading. "You are a tough crowd."

Turning around to face the chief, Liv smoothed her black hooded cape. "Trock Swaliswan, how many times have you been politely warned not to steal from the mortals on this island?"

The goblin struggled in his bindings, making him roll more into the mud and eat a mouthful of dirt.

"Oops, sorry." Liv lifted her hand, and the goblin rose and stood upright. "That's better."

Trock spat out a mouthful of mud, splattering Liv's boots. She eyed it and gave the goblin a disgusted look. "I'm going to allow that to pass this one time. The next time, you lose an ear."

The goblin laughed, showing a mouthful of missing or blackened teeth. "You're a joke if the House of Seven sent you to deal with us. They know we can't be stopped."

Liv tipped her finger to the side and the goblin's face flew forward, his feet still connected to the Earth. She stood him back up after drenching his face in mud once more. "The thing is, I'm new to the House, and darn it if I know how to play by the rules." She spun, and her cape swirled around her. With the movement, the closest small huts crumbled to the ground.

When she faced the chief again, Liv slapped her hand to her forehead. "Oops. Did I do that? Sorry."

The goblin shook his head, mud spraying in all directions but missing Liv. "You're not to damage our property when enforcing rules."

11

"Right, I'm supposed to cite you for your injustices," Liv agreed in a bored voice. "Tell you that this is a warning, and if you do it again, you'll have to answer to the Council and possibly have your magic locked." Liv yawned loudly. "Here's the thing: you don't care about those punishments. You're going to keep doing this until someone teaches you not to, so I figured I'd save everyone the trouble and be that person."

"This is not how the rules work!" Trock yelled.

Liv dared take a step forward, her hand in front of her, and pointed at the chief's chest with a murderous look in her eyes. "You dare to speak of rules when you don't follow them?"

"We're protected by the agreement set by the House of Seven," Trock argued. "You can't harm me! That was the agreement when we submitted to having our magic governed by the House."

Liv looked around casually. "Thing is, I don't see anyone here to stop me." She twitched one finger to the side and the ropes around the goblin tightened, making his face instantly grow a shade darker. The goblins around them shrank back from the sight. Liv took another step forward. "Now, this is how it's going to go under *my* law. You're going to stop stealing from mortals; no more taking their possessions. As stated in the agreement, you can have that which is lost or discarded, but under no circumstances are you to steal anymore. Do you understand?"

The goblin sneered at her, his large eyes bulging.

"Look, I get that words are hard, so a simple yes will suffice," Liv said, still pointing her finger in Trock's direction.

His expression didn't change.

She nodded calmly. "Very well." Liv swept her free hand at a row of squatty huts, sending them straight to the ground. Around her many of the goblins screamed with grief, running for the rubble of their houses.

Liv held her hand out to another row of huts, probably filled with innocent people's stolen goods. "Tell me, Trock, how long will it take you all to rebuild if I destroy everything?"

"Don't!" the chief yelled, hopping forward in his bindings. "We will stop! I promise!"

Liv gave him a skeptical stare. "Are you sure? I know how hard it is for you goblins to behave yourselves."

Furiously the chief shook his head. "We will follow the agreement. You have my word. And we'll return the goods we stole. Just leave here without doing any more damage."

Liv nodded. "I'll do you one better." She swept her arm through the air, and the huts she'd destroyed rose back into place as if they'd never been demolished.

Scratchy whispers issued from the goblins as they marveled at the magic. Goblins' magic was restricted to finding spells like the ones that helped them locate the riches they'd stolen that day, and those fireballs they could throw. They didn't have powers close to those of the magicians, and rebuilding their houses would have taken a long time.

Liv rounded on the chief, giving him a serious look. She nodded once and the ropes binding him fell away. "Now, do as you promised, and return the items you stole."

Trock shook out his stumpy limbs and cracked his neck. "It's getting late, magician. We'll do it tomorrow."

Liv sighed, rolling her eyes. "That's not what we agreed upon. I guess I'll have to unleash my kitty on you."

From the darkened jungle on the other side of the closest hut, the sound of a furious lion roaring echoed through the camp, jolting the ground and making the leaves quake.

The goblins all hopped from their places, grabbing the various stolen objects and hurrying off to return them as if they had fireballs chasing them.

It's not fire, but it will do, Liv thought as she watched them scurrying around.

CHAPTER THREE

"Crack two eggs into a mixing bowl," Liv read from the recipe book on her countertop.

She took an egg from the carton and cracked it against the bowl with a bit too much force, knocking bits of shell in with it. "Oops. How do you get the eggshell back out?"

Plato looked up from where he was sitting on a mountain of junk on the countertop. "You keep it out in the first place."

Liv dismissed him with a shake of her head. "That's not very helpful, but you already knew that." She dumped the egg into the sink and tried cracking another one. This time she was successful.

"So, although I like the mystery of never knowing what I'll find when I sit on a heap of stuff," Plato began, looking around, "I was thinking you might want to consider cleaning up the place."

Liv gazed around at her studio apartment, which looked more like a war zone than a place where someone lived. "I'm due at work in less than an hour, and I still need to practice the disguising spell Rory taught me. When do I have time?"

"Well, don't waste your energy using magic to clean the place, especially since you haven't eaten anything yet and your reserves are low."

Pulling out all three of the drawers in her kitchen, Liv looked around furiously for a whisk. The oil in the pan was nearly too hot. "And it looks like I might starve at this rate. Who knew that cooking was so hard?"

"You know that you don't have to cook all of your meals," Plato reminded her.

She grabbed a fork and began whipping the eggs. "I'm tired of eating from the bakery down the street. I need my leather pants to fit, or I'll have to get a bigger cape to hide my ass."

"Magicians who regularly practice magic are rarely overweight, and a Warrior shouldn't have any problems at all."

Liv nodded. One of the best benefits of being a magician was that she wouldn't get fat. "Honestly, I just want to try to be a bit more self-sufficient. It would be nice not to eat out for every meal. And it's getting expensive."

"You could be eating at the House of Seven," Plato stated.

Liv grimaced. "Then I'd have to talk to people, and I'm pretty sure that might kill me."

"You like talking to *some* people," he observed.

Liv poured the half-beaten eggs into the pan, making the oil crackle and pop. "She's different."

Plato stretched, causing a pile of overdue bills to slide to the floor. They landed on a heap of dirty laundry.

"Hey now, I had that sorted just the way I like it," Liv grumbled.

"Speaking of food." Plato looked around. "Have you seen my food dish? It seems to have gotten lost in the shuffle."

Liv pursed her lips, pushing aside grocery bags and dishes on the counter. "Yeah, sorry about that. I really do need to clean up this place. I just don't know when I'll have the time. Rory insists that I sleep, which means I have time for little else when I'm out fighting goblins who steal trinkets and chasing down minotaurs who track mud through the streets of Spain or whatever other trivial cases the Councilors assign me."

Plato pushed his nose into another stack of papers, making most of them fall to the ground. He relished when he found his food bowl but frowned when he discovered it was empty.

Liv's mouth dropped open. "Oh, sorry. I forgot to get you food. I'll do that today. Do you want some of my eggs?"

Plato sniffed the air. "I don't like burned food."

"Burned?" Liv looked up and ran over to the stove, where her eggs were smoking. "Damn it! When did taking care of myself and you get to be so hard?"

Plato jumped off the counter and disappeared into the pantry. "I'll be okay. I can always find something."

Liv turned off the burner and began scraping the eggs into the trash can. Those had been her last eggs, which meant there wasn't anything else in the apartment that was edible. Well, besides the cat...

She giggled to herself when a red velvet bag tied with a drawstring appeared atop the pile of disorganized junk on the countertop. Liv halted, regarding the bag with hesitation.

"Ummm… I think I got a package, but I didn't order anything," Liv said, sliding the still-hot pan into the sink.

Plato exited the pantry carrying a roasted drumstick in his mouth. He eyed the package and then set to work gnawing on the meat.

"Hey, where'd you get that?" Liv asked, looking down at the feline.

"Magic," he told her coyly.

Liv thought about asking for half but shook her head instead. "So, do you think whatever is in the bag is safe?"

"Well, did it magically appear out of nowhere?"

"Yes."

"And were you expecting anything from anyone?"

"No."

"Do you have any enemies?"

"Yes."

"Then probably it's not." Plato went back to work tearing the skin off the drumstick, which had steam rising off of it like it was still hot.

Liv gave the cat a reluctant expression. "I don't get you, Plato. You're a very strange animal." She came around the kitchen bar and regarded the bag with a long stare, expecting a goblin to jump out and try to punch her in the face. When nothing happened, she poked the bag and waited. Still nothing.

Finally, too curious, Liv pulled at the drawstrings of the bag, opening it. "Here goes nothing," she said, plunging her hand in. The thick papery material that greeted her hand was a complete surprise. Liv knew that sensation but hadn't felt it in a while. She was holding a wad of cash when she pulled her hand from the bag.

"Who sent this?" she asked, looking at the hundreds of dollars nestled in her hand.

"I'm guessing the House of Seven," Plato replied. "It must be payday."

"House of Seven?" Liv asked, setting the money on the counter next to the ever-growing pile of mail and bills. She dug into the bag again and found one more slip of paper. This one wasn't as thick, and on it was written Weekly Earnings for Liv Beaufont.

Her jaw hung open as she regarded the piece of paper and then the money. "I've been paid."

"Well, you didn't think it was a volunteer position, did you?"

"I mean, I knew they'd pay me, but I guess I expected leprechaun gold or gems or something else worthless in the real world. I never expected cash."

"They live in this world too, you know."

Liv grabbed the money and counted it properly, relishing in the excitement of having so much of it. "Yeah, but it doesn't really feel like it. The Councilors and Warriors all seem like they are from a different world than the one we live in."

"They do reside in a different one, but theirs is actually in *our* world. Never forget that. They can't get away from our world, which is why they are bound to protect it."

Liv regarded Plato for a moment, wondering what else he knew that he wasn't saying. It would do no good to pry. He was a vault when he wanted to be.

"Well, it looks like I can buy us an actual breakfast," Liv

said, pocketing the money. "I'll also buy you some cat food on the way home from work. And catch up on my bills for once."

Plato chewed on a piece of meat. "May I also suggest that you use that money to make your life a little easier?"

"I don't think this is enough money to rid the world of Bianca Mantovani and her constant disapproving stares and remarks."

Plato snorted with laughter. "I'm afraid it isn't. But I was actually thinking you could use it to hire a maid. Since you refuse to quit your shift at John's shop, you need to farm out some of your other responsibilities."

"Yeah, that's not a bad idea," Liv said, looking around at the chaos and disorder that was once her safe haven, the first home she'd made for herself after her parents' death. "And I guess I'll get paid regularly, and this is way more than I make working for John."

"Which means…" Plato took a long, hard look at the kitchen, "that you can also afford to hire someone to cook for us, since you can't do it."

"Hey, I could have magicked us some food," Liv argued.

Plato shook his head. "I'm afraid not. Remember that with domestic magic, if you don't know how to do something, it's that much harder when using magic."

"Right, so if I don't know how to play the cello, then using magic won't necessarily make it so that I can," Liv stated.

Plato nodded. "Magic makes your life easier, but it doesn't replace skill."

"But I did control the wind last night, which was pretty cool."

"That's elemental magic," Plato stated. "Also remember that there are many different types of magic, and they cross over and their rules bleed together, which means—"

Liv nodded, cutting him off. "That magic is one complicated beast."

CHAPTER FOUR

S taring at the red coils of the toaster, Liv waited to see what Beth Dallas was talking about. The IT expert had brought the toaster back to the shop after it had been repaired, saying it was doing something bizarre.

Her Dalmatian, Jersey Girl, was currently running her snout along the bottom shelf, trying to find Plato.

"Jers, give it a rest," Liv said, turning around to scold the dog.

The dog gave her a scornful expression as she backed away.

Liv was only looking out for Jersey Girl. The last time she didn't let up on Plato, her spots all mysteriously disappeared, freaking out both the dog and Beth. Liv had made up a lie that it was common for Dalmatians to lose their spots. Thankfully they had come back, and Beth wasn't asking any more questions.

The toaster popped. "See there?" Beth exclaimed.

Liv turned to find two pieces of toast bouncing in the

toaster, perfectly crisp on both sides. "So, it works? That's not strange."

"I didn't put any bread in there," Beth explained, pulling the warm toast out and showing it to Liv.

"Maybe you forgot…" Liv tried, her face growing warm. She'd repaired Beth's toaster herself, and Beth was on a list of clients who had toasters that worked without bread or microwaves that always had fresh popcorn when their owner opened the door to heat up tea. Damage control was getting more difficult, the more things she repaired.

"No, just watch. It does it every time." Beth pushed down the lever on the toaster, but Liv knew what was going to happen next.

"This isn't weird," Liv said, lacing her words with the magical influence she'd learned to use when dealing with the other customers.

Beth looked up. Her face brightened. "Yeah, you know, you're right. This is totally normal."

The technique didn't always work, and Rory had said it was most helpful on mortals. The giant had actually been surprised that Liv had the power of "influence."

"Still, let me do some tweaking on it to ensure it's working properly," Liv said, pulling up the lever and watching as two almost-cooked pieces of bread popped up. "Maybe you can come back tomorrow sometime?"

Beth nodded, slapping her leg to get Jersey Girl's attention. "Yes, that sounds good." The two left, both looking slightly dazed.

"What did you do to the dog?" Liv asked, turning around to face the shelf.

Plato's black and white head poked out from between a

handheld vacuum and a humidifier. "I did the same thing you did to Beth."

"What did you influence Jersey Dog to think?"

"That she's a cat."

Liv rolled her eyes, but she laughed as she turned back to the toaster. "I've got to figure out how to stop doing this stuff to devices. Either that or I'm going back to repairing stuff the old-fashioned way."

"I think it will have to be a combination of both."

Liv nodded. "Yeah, I remember. Find out what's wrong with the device first, then tailor the magic to fix that specific thing." Liv thought for a moment before directing her attention back to Plato, who was squeezing out from between the appliances. "Hey, why is it that I can't cook food with magic but I can make toasters that produce endless amounts of bread? And I have to know how to do something to use magic to do it, but I can make these devices do all this strange and awesome stuff?"

Plato jumped up on the workbench. "Magic is unpredictable when you mix it with technology. Remember what Rory told you to do before you could control your power?"

"Stay away from tech," Liv answered.

"That's right, because technology has its own brand of magic which, when mixed with yours, has assorted effects."

Liv laughed. "Technology is science, not magic."

Plato sniffed at the toast. "Science and magic are the same thing. It's just that one is understood and the other isn't."

"You seem to understand magic, at least a little more than you let on at times," Liv observed.

Plato pretended he hadn't heard the statement. "What

SARAH NOFFKE & MICHAEL ANDERLE

are you going to tell John if he finds out about these appliances?"

Liv pulled the toaster closer to take a better look at it. "Well, I'm not using that brainwashing technique or whatever it is on him."

"I think he's growing suspicious of you, though."

Liv let out an exasperated sigh. "I know he is, but I don't know what to do about it."

"Have you thought about telling him the truth?" Plato offered.

"Only a hundred times," Liv said as she pulled the bottom off the toaster. "My mother, when she was younger, had a friend who lived next door to her. They grew up together, and although my mother grew up in a family of magicians, they hid it, as the House encourages. Well, one day she decided she was going to tell her best friend the truth. Tell her that she was a magician and she could do weird and wonderful things."

"I don't have to hear how the story ended, because it's been written a hundred times in history books," Plato said, his voice suddenly morose.

Liv sighed, pushing the toaster away, defeated. "Yes, magicians have been persecuted from the beginning. Or their powers are dismissed as alien activity or some other phenomenon."

"You know that's for the best," Plato told her simply.

"I don't, actually." Liv gazed around the store, her second home, feeling a sense of loss. "How is it that we operate separately from the mortals, hiding who we truly are? It doesn't make any sense."

"And yet, that's how it's been for quite some time."

"Has it always been that way?" Liv asked.

Plato gave her an offended look. "How am I supposed to know?"

"Because you've been around since the dawning of the ages," Liv replied with a dry laugh.

"Is that what that book Rory gave you says?"

Liv shrugged. "It says that you Lynxes have many lives, and that's supposedly where the old wives' tale that cats have nine lives came from."

"Don't believe everything you read, dear Liv."

"So it's *not* true, then?"

Plato laid his head down on his paws as the front door opened. Pickles, John's terrier, ran in first, yelping at the cat. John shook his head, raindrops flicking off his hair as he did.

"The people in LA act like rain is acid and they can't venture out in it," he commented, pulling off his coat.

"They will melt, you know," Liv said with a laugh.

"Yes, their powdered noses and big hair will probably melt if they go outside in the rain." John's eye caught the toaster in front of Liv. "I thought you repaired Beth's toaster?"

"I did, but apparently I need to take another look at it."

John nodded. "Did she ever figure out what happened to Jersey Girl's spots?" John asked, pulling a treat out of his pocket and offering it to Pickles to get him to settle down.

Liv went back to work on the toaster, avoiding John's gaze. "Just a fluke. She's fine now." *Besides from the fact that she thinks she's a cat,* Liv thought.

"I noticed that a few things came back after you

repaired them," John said, angling to the shelf where the microwave sat. "Is everything all right?"

This was her chance—her chance to tell him that she was a magician and she'd been messing up appliance repairs. Well, making the appliances better than they should be. But then her mother's words rang in her head, "Mortals want to accept us, but for some reason, they usually can't. It's a mystery. It's almost like they have been forbidden from doing so. Our magic doesn't fit in their world."

Liv bit down on her lip. "Everything is fine. I just rushed the repairs on the microwave and toaster, but I'll fix it. I promise."

John looked at her sideways but then nodded, not looking entirely convinced. "And that other job of yours? How's that going?"

Why did he have to care so much? Liv didn't like lying to him, but she didn't see another way. Maybe Rory would have some insights she could borrow. As soon as she thought of the giant, he appeared at the front door, although she didn't remember seeing him walk past the front glass, and strangely, he wasn't covered in rain like John. Of course, it wasn't really strange since she knew how mysterious magic was, but it still gave her chills every time she witnessed it.

John followed Liv's line of sight, his face brightening. "Well, hey there, Rory! I didn't hear you come in! You're as quiet as a mouse."

"Yes, but built like a rhino," Liv teased. "How do you pull off such stealth?"

Rory gave a nervous chuckle. "It must have been the rain."

"Yes, but you must have moved fast enough to miss most of the sprinkles, huh?" Liv questioned.

John looked Rory over. "Yeah, you don't have a drop on you."

"That mouse-like behavior must let you sprint around raindrops," Liv said.

John looked back at Liv, a perplexed expression on his face. "It *is* quite strange."

Rory shot her an annoyed look.

"Oh, I bet you jumped between the awnings, didn't you?" Liv supplied.

The giant nodded. "Indeed I did."

So, Rory was keen to keep his magic a secret, too. There was more for her to learn on this subject.

John clapped his hands together, making Pickles bark. "Well, my boy, what did you bring me today? I still can't believe all the treasure you gave me yesterday. They look mighty fine on the shelf." He held up his hand, proudly indicating the row of devices Rory had dropped off yesterday, saying it was junk he had found in the yard.

He shook his head of curly brown hair. "I don't have anything yet, but I'm working on some stuff." His face turned an interesting shade of pink. "Actually, I'm here to ask for services."

John beamed. "Oh, well, that's what we do. Repair the stuff we don't want you to throw out and fill the landfills with. Where's your device?"

Rory slipped his hands into his pockets. "It's too big for

me to bring in. My mum's refrigerator has gone out in the house."

"Oh, I love a good house call," John exclaimed, his eyes dancing with eagerness. "And refrigerators are my favorite."

"Actually, I was hoping that Liv could help with this one," Rory said, his eyes on the ground.

Pickles, who had been scratching furiously, stopped and looked up at the giant at the same time as his master. "Liv?"

"Well, it's just that…" Rory trailed away, his voice and face guilty.

"That I've been begging to test my experience repairing refrigerators and this would be the perfect chance," Liv offered.

"You have?" John asked, scratching his head.

"Yes," Liv said at once. "I told Rory that the other day. Thanks for remembering, pal."

The guilt melted off the giant's face. "Yeah, I remembered."

"Oh, well, you haven't had much chance to work on refrigerators, and it's a mighty useful skill," John stated. "Yes, it's a good idea for you to go. You're small, so it will probably be easier for you to work on those old-model refrigerators. But I want you to call me if you run into any issues. It can be a complicated repair." John stopped and thought for a moment. "We could both go, actually—"

"No," Rory cut in.

When John turned to look at him, the giant forced a wide smile. "I mean, I'd hate to take you both away from the shop for this repair. I already feel bad enough asking for a house call."

John waved him off. "I owe you tons for all the valuable merchandise you've put on my shelves. I wished you'd let me pay you for it."

"Yeah, Rory, why do you refuse to allow anyone to pay you for the stuff?" Liv asked, starting to catch onto the giant's act and enjoying making him squirm.

"I just happen across those appliances and stuff while browsing," Rory explained. "It's not anything I need, but I don't want it going to waste. It's a win-win for us all."

Liv smiled behind John's back. She knew the giant was up to something with all his deeds, but she couldn't figure out what. Was he actually like the good fairy of the giant world? She wasn't sure, but she was going to find out.

"All right, let me grab my coat and toolbox and I'll follow you over to your place," Liv said as Plato stretched to a standing position, waking from his nap. "And maybe you can show me how to jump from awning to awning so that I don't get wet either."

CHAPTER FIVE

"Are you real proud of yourself?" Rory asked as he tried to squeeze into the back of the SUV.

Liv had asked him why they didn't just teleport or use whatever "weird-giant-travel" he had at his disposal, but he'd shook her off, muttering about how it wasn't a good idea to risk it.

She watched with amusement as he tried to find a place to put his long legs. After about a minute of this shuffling, Liv jumped into the backseat of the SUV beside him and stretched out, her short legs having plenty of space to kick around.

He eyed her with brooding contempt. "I'll remember this the next time you can't reach something off a low shelf."

"Ha-ha." Liv giggled. "And yes, making you squirm in front of John gave my life new meaning, so thanks for that."

"You need a hobby, I think."

Liv yawned. "I need a nap, is what I need."

Rory gave her a considering look as the driver pulled the vehicle onto the road and immediately into bumper to bumper traffic.

"Oh, don't worry, Grandma." Liv waved off his concern. "I'm getting plenty of sleep and eating my vegetables."

"It would serve you better if you were eating carbs," Rory advised. "They keep you fuller longer."

"Then I'll pick up nachos after this," Liv said, already salivating. "And hey, where are we going, by the way? I'm guessing you don't have a refrigerator you need repaired."

Rory shook his head and pulled a few bills from his pocket and handed them to Liv. "No, but pretend that you did and give this to John for the repairs. I'll report back to him later that you did an adequate job."

Liv slid the money into her bag. "How about we change that adjective to 'superb job'"

Rory shook his head. "I want him to believe the lie."

Liv scowled at the giant. "By the way, you lie to him about...well, you know." She cut her eyes at the driver.

"Don't worry," Rory stated. "I put a sound spell on the vehicle. He thinks we're riding in complete silence."

"Damn, that was fast. So he can't hear me if I scream or start singing at the top of my lungs?"

Rory nodded. "And he won't know if I throw you out of the vehicle. Well, not until it's too late."

"Okay, so then tell me, why don't you tell mortals about your magic? Like John, for instance?"

Rory thought for a moment, his green eyes scrutinizing the road ahead. "It's not safe for them to know."

"I don't understand," Liv said when he'd been quiet for a long moment.

"I don't understand it myself, but it has never worked for mortals to know about magic," Rory explained. "They either rebel against it or dive so far into the idea that they harm themselves. Mostly, their first instincts are to dismiss the idea as false."

"That's understandable, actually," Liv stated. "I don't know if I'd believe it either, in their position."

"Yes, but magic is real," Rory said. "But even when confronted with proof, mortals usually deny it, and this causes bigger problems."

"How so?"

Rory's face turned dark. "I don't know. It's just always been dangerous for mortals to know about magic. It seems to make them insane and alienates them from society."

"Like the crazy old woman who swears she sees things and no one believes her?" Liv asked.

"Yes, something like that."

"Well, then I'm glad I haven't told John."

Rory watched the traffic on the road as if watching for something. Without looking at Liv, he said, "John might be able to take the news. I don't know. But you shouldn't tell him anything unless it becomes absolutely necessary. It's just not worth the risk."

"I think that was what my instincts told me," Liv agreed with a nod.

"Always listen to your instincts. They're never wrong."

"So, since I'm not fixing your refrigerator, where are you taking me?"

"You'll see when we get there."

Liv raised an eyebrow at the giant. "Wow, you're an

35

awful tour guide. This is the last excursion I'm going on with you."

"Why don't you take a nap until we get there?" Rory suggested, and there was something in his tone that Liv couldn't resist. She found her eyelids immediately falling shut.

What seemed like only a few seconds later, Rory was shaking her back awake.

"Hey, wake up. We're here," Rory said as the vehicle slowed.

Liv startled and sat up. "Wait, what? I fell asleep? How did that happen?"

Rory pointed at her mouth. "I have no idea, but you're drooling all over the place."

Liv shot him a skeptical look as she dragged her sleeve across her mouth. "I think you *do* have an idea, and it's all related to your weird-giant-magic ways."

"Come on," Rory said, opening the SUV's back door. "I have something I want to show you."

Liv popped out of the other door, peering around at the busy street they were parked on. When she came around the vehicle, Rory was still struggling to get out of the back seat.

"I thought you said you wanted to show me something?" Liv asked, suppressing a laugh. "Was it this contortionist stunt? Because it's not as entertaining as you think."

Rory's legs were stuck behind the driver's side. He leaned to the side, nearly falling over in the seat and wiggled his way out, pulling his legs out first and then his torso.

Once he was fully out of the SUV, he steered Liv in the direction of a large building.

"The Natural History Museum?" Liv asked when he'd finally released her. "You're taking me on a field trip?"

Rory told her as they walked up a long set of stairs, "There's something inside that I need to show you."

"I've seen dinosaur bones," Liv told him, having to run to keep up with him. "They aren't that cool."

"And what they have here aren't the real dinosaur bones anyway," Rory stated.

"How do you know that?"

"Because they were destroyed long ago in one of the great wars," Rory explained.

"Great wars?" Liv asked.

"It's a part of giant history."

"Then if these aren't the real bones, what do they have on display here?"

"The bones of things that aren't yet extinct."

"Wait, there are still dinosaurs roaming around?" Liv asked.

"Well, you know them better as dragons, but yes."

"Why didn't I learn about any of this, or about this great war? I did have several years of education while I was growing up in the House of Seven, although mine was a bit more organic than most."

Rory continued through the glass doors, breezing past the security guards, who didn't seem to notice him.

"Miss," an employee of the museum said, stopping Liv as she tried to pass. "I'm going to need to see your ticket."

Liv halted, watching as Rory continued into the massive hall. "Ummm, I don't have one."

The employee pointed to her hand. "Of course you do. It's right there. I just need to scan it."

Liv looked down at her hand. She was indeed holding a paper ticket, although she didn't remember how it got there. "Right," she said, handing it to the employee.

A moment later, after she'd been allowed entry, she hurried to catch up with Rory. "Another clever trick, Decepticon."

"And to answer your last question, there is much that the House doesn't acknowledge from the history books. It will be your job to learn as much of the history as you can despite them."

"Is that why we're here? Are you going to teach some of it to me?"

Rory cut around a group of chatting school kids. "I don't even know all of the history. Yes, I know the parts that pertain to giants and some other magical races, but most of it wasn't documented well. The magicians' history, for instance, has many holes in it."

That struck Liv as strange. She'd never heard this about her history, but she'd always had a feeling that many things had been left out of the magicians' textbooks. Her parents had said as much to her when she was growing up. That was one reason they had resisted formal education for their children, instead encouraging them to explore to find knowledge. "The most valuable knowledge can't be found in a textbook, but rather in the places you are told never to look," her father had told her repeatedly. That rebellious spirit had often gotten him into trouble, and now...well, he was dead. Still, Liv, knowing what she knew now, would rather follow her parents' path and risk it all than live a safe life following a cookie-cutter route.

"And I am here to show you a bit of history, although your education will come purely as a by-product to my agenda," Rory said, abruptly turning into a corridor that wasn't as congested as the others.

"Wow, you have quite the way with words," Liv said, noticing a group of elderly women giving her strange stares as they passed. "What's their problem? Is my mascara smeared on my face from sleeping?" She ran her fingers under her eyes in an attempt to clean up her makeup.

Rory paused, turning in a complete circle as if he was momentarily lost. "What do you mean?"

"Why are people looking at me so strangely?" Liv asked after he resumed walking.

"Besides the fact that you're a runt who they think has gotten separated from her school group?"

"Yes, besides that," Liv replied with a laugh.

"Well, it looks as though you're talking to yourself since they can't see me."

"But *I* can see you."

Rory gave her a sideways look and winked. "Yes. It's called selective disguise."

"Very sneaky. Remind me never to trust a giant. Wait, don't remind me. I remember now; I don't trust you."

"We're not as sneaky as your lynx, and you trust him," Rory said, stopping in front of an archway to a darkened room.

"Plato isn't... Yeah, well, you are both sneaks."

Rory wasn't paying attention to her anymore. His eyes

were focused on a case in the middle of the next room. He held up a hand and pointed at it. "In there."

Liv trotted forward, trying to make out what was in the oversized case. When she stepped into the room, a sharp chill ran down her spine. She turned to find that Rory hadn't moved. "Hey, aren't you coming?"

He shook his head. "I can't."

"'Can't?'" Liv questioned. "I get that you'll have to duck to get under that arch, but that's no lower than the front door to John's shop."

Rory shook his head again. "No, there's something that prevents me from entering that particular room."

Liv looked over her shoulder and then back at the giant. "Oh, well, then that must mean…" She stepped forward, glad she had the room to herself as she neared the large horizontal case. Lying on a white surface under thick glass was a huge sword. Liv had never seen anything like it. The hilt was cast in bronze and wrapped with a leather grip, and the blade was so shiny that it nearly hurt her eyes to look directly at it. The carvings on the hilt were incredibly detailed, and the sheath lying beside the sword was covered in hundreds of rubies.

She read the placard beside the display. "Thought to be from the Roman empire. Circa unknown."

Liv turned around, aware that her mouth was hanging open. "This didn't belong to the Romans, did it?"

Rory's eyes were glazed when he shook his head.

"This is a giant's sword, isn't it?" Liv asked, thinking that only someone as tall as Rory could swing such a large weapon.

Again the giant nodded.

"But why can't you come in here?"

"That, I don't know," Rory answered. "It's been that way since this museum was built over a hundred years ago."

"But this museum is run by mortals. And what is the sword doing in the Natural History Museum anyway?" Liv asked.

Rory let out a long breath. "Unfortunately, in all this time we've been able to uncover no information on the mystery. The sword belonged to my grandfather, Rory Bemuth Laurens. It is called 'Turbinger.' It disappeared long ago, then showed up here with magical wards around it that prevented us giants from taking it back."

"So you can't go near it, but I can?"

"It appears so," Rory answered. "Although this was the first time I had the chance to test the notion."

"That must mean that magicians have put a protective spell on the sword," Liv ventured.

Rory didn't look so sure. "Maybe, but magicians like to keep things hidden for their eyes only. You probably have an entire museum of artifacts in the House of Seven."

Liv thought about the library where she used to spend many an evening. It was more of a treasure vault of strange objects than a place to find books. "So, mortals have your grandfather's sword, but who put the wards around it to prevent you from taking it back?"

"Again, this is all unclear," Rory stated. "All I know is that the sword that should belong to my family and me has been on display in this room for a century, with no way for us to reclaim it."

Liv found herself frowning. "That's sad. I'm sorry."

"Giants are known for their superior metal work," Rory

explained. "My grandfather, one of the most talented craftsmen I've ever known, made this sword. It isn't just incredibly strong and never dulls, but it has also been imbued with unique magic that protects the bearer."

"Damn, I'd like a sword like that," Liv said, running her eyes over the beautiful weapon lying in the case.

"And you could have one," Rory said with an edge to his voice.

Liv spun around. "I could?"

"I could make you your very own sword, one that was fit for you and your stature."

"You mean, tiny," Liv said with a laugh.

"Real swords are created specifically for the person. My grandfather knew how to craft them so they complimented the one who wielded them. That skill has since died out, though."

"But I bet you still know how to do it," Liv stated.

Rory nodded. "Yes. He taught me everything I know, and I'd be willing to make you a sword—one that was an extension of you, and stronger and more beautiful than any sword any magician has ever used."

Liv looked back at the sword before facing Rory directly. "You've got my attention. What's the catch?"

The giant grinned slightly. "I only ask a favor of you in return for this sword I'd make for you."

"Go on," Liv encouraged, her tone dry.

"All you have to is to steal my grandfather's sword from where it's being held right now."

Liv blinked at the giant dully. "Right, you want me to break into a nationally-famed museum. That's *all* I have to do."

CHAPTER SIX

L iv ran her hand over the walls in the entrance hall and watched as the ancient symbols lit up and danced under her fingertips. She stared at them each time she came to the House of Seven, feeling as though they were yearning to tell her a message. The harder she looked at the symbols, the more familiar they seemed, and yet the meaning was never revealed to her.

"Can you believe what he wants me to do?" she asked Plato, who was beside her, referring to Rory's request for her to steal the sword. Plato had apparently been lurking in the shadows of the museum the entire time, so he knew what Rory was asking of her.

"It sounds like a perfectly reasonable arrangement," Plato said, strolling with his tail high. "You need a weapon, and he needs a favor, which you can provide."

"Who said I needed a weapon?"

"Well, wind and intimidation are fine for fighting goblins, but one day your adversaries are going to be taller than knee-height."

Liv agreed with a nod. "Hey, I did pretty well with putting that minotaur in his place, if you remember correctly."

"Yes, but you used a long red scarf to distract him," Plato responded.

"All so I could corral him out of the streets of Spain. I really hope the Councilors don't assign me another shitty case like that."

"Well, at least the mortals thought the minotaur was a bull, and no one was the wiser after you got him out of there," Plato said.

"I'm not certain that the mortals would know they were looking at a unicorn even if it stuck its horn up their—"

"Barn-side," Plato offered, cutting in.

"Yes, that was exactly what I was going to say. 'Barn-side.'"

"Mortals see what they expect to see, but faced with too much magic, the blinders will come off," Plato advised.

"Rory said something about how it's not safe for mortals to know about magic. Do you think that's true?" Liv asked.

"I think it's complicated, and it depends on who you ask," Plato answered. "For magicians and giants and many other magical creatures, it's probably better if mortals don't know about all the happenings in the magical world. However, I'm not sure how mortals would feel about it."

"Because they've never been asked?" Liv posed.

Plato nodded. "I suspect as much."

"Well, here in the magical community, we're excellent at deciding what's good for everyone else," Liv said as she rounded the corner to face the Door of Reflection. Her image stared back at her, rippling like the surface of the door was made of water. Her long, flowing blonde hair was mostly tucked under the black hood of her cape, which hung down her back.

Liv pretended that the black void to her left wasn't drawing her attention. Lately, when she looked down the corridor into the chasm of darkness, she felt a strange pull toward it. But much like the white tiger and black crow, no one talked about this strange aspect of the House of Seven. The magicians usually hurried past it, not even noticing that they were striding by something that looked like a cliff leading off the edge of the world.

Stepping through the Door of Reflection, Liv allowed herself to move forward, now accustomed to the strange feeling of passing into the Chamber of the Tree. The process was supposed to cleanse the member of Seven of fears and doubts before each meeting. Liv didn't understand why she always experienced a strange dream where she was going blind and was surrounded by indistinct figures.

She expected to see that same dream as she passed through the door, but it was different. Liv was standing on the edge of a mountain, eerily similar to the one she imagined her parents fell from to their deaths five years prior. The wind whipped at her back, sending cold shivers over her skin. In the distance, she spotted smoke rising from what appeared to be a cozy village. The smoke quickly turned into raging flames that spread from rooftop to rooftop. Liv startled, feeling like she was the only one for miles who could see the fire. The only one who could help. But she was too far away, imprisoned on a mountain peak.

Stumbling through the Door of Reflection, Liv straightened as soon as her current reality took shape. She pushed her shoulders back and raised her chin high, trying to disguise the remnants of what she'd just seen.

The Councilors all sat in their usual places on the high semi-circular bench at the back of the chamber. Also as usual, not all of the Warriors were present, most were off working their cases. Maria Rosario, Stefan Ludwig, and Decar Sinclair stood with their backs to Liv, their focus on the Councilors.

Silently, Liv took her place between Decar and Stefan.

"Ms. Rosario, do you feel you can handle this case alone?" Adler Sinclair asked, his light-colored eyes briefly flicking to Liv.

"I'm confident that I can intervene before the poison gets into the water supply," Maria stated with assurance. She wore a beautifully embroidered maroon jacket, her long black hair cascading down her back.

"You must be swift," Adler warned. "The lives of thousands are in your hands."

The Warrior nodded and pivoted, striding quickly for the exit.

The attention of the Councilors shifted, most looking at Decar, although Liv received a quick glance from Clark.

"The rebellion between the Elves," Adler began, "Has it been quelled yet?"

"I need to meet with more of their diplomats and smooth over some boundary issues," Decar answered. "But I think that within a fortnight, we'll have come to an agreement."

Adler nodded, looking around at his peers. "I think

that's reasonable, considering what's at stake. I approve the next steps of the negotiation."

There was a communal agreement from the rest of the Councilors, and much like Maria, Decar spun and marched away.

"Ms. Beaufont..." Adler began, his voice suddenly sounding tired as he reviewed the tablet of notes in front of him.

"Very creative problem solving," Hester DeVries stated, a kind smile spreading on her face. "The goblins actually returned many of the stolen items, is that right?"

Liv nearly snorted with laughter. "Well, they didn't want to at first, but I was able to persuade them that it would be in their best interests."

Adler pressed his fingertips to his forehead, that typical annoyed look on his pale face. "Ms. Beaufont, you tied up Chief Trock Swaliswan, humiliating him in front of his entire tribe."

"*That* was what humiliated him?" Liv asked. "You should have seen the ridiculous getup he was wearing. I mostly covered him in ropes to save my eyes from being set on fire."

From the corner of Liv's eyes, she saw a faint smile crack Stefan's face. His sister, Raina Ludwig, also looked quite amused. She was sitting between Hester and Clark on the bench.

Adler tapped his fingers impatiently on the table in front of him.

"I think that you, Olivia, need some lessons in diplomacy," Bianca Mantovani offered, her sharp cheekbones looking hollow in the twinkling light the tree cast down on her. She read from her tablet, shaking her head with disapproval. "Is it true that you threw several goblins across the camp area?"

Liv laughed. "Name's Liv. And the little heathens were about to poke me with dull blades and pitchforks. I believe that's called defending myself."

The white tiger strode around the bench, looking even more majestic than Liv remembered. He didn't glance at her, but rather stalked around the circumference of the room, his head held high. *What the hell was up with that animal, and why did no one seem to give him much notice?* Liv wondered. *Just a giant cat strolling through the chamber. Nothing to see here.*

"I don't see what the problem with Liv's tactics was," Raina said, her voice clear and loud. "A Warrior is permitted to use whatever defensive measures are required in a case such as this. And although goblins aren't considered lethal magical creatures, in large numbers such as these, they can be overwhelming."

Haro Takahashi and Lorenzo Rosario agreed with a nod, but Bianca ignored Raina's words, leaning forward to look down the bench at Raina.

"The problem is that Olivia's tactics have created extra problems for the House," she explained.

Raina was undeterred and pointed up at the tree, on whose branches each of the Councilors' and Warriors' names glowed brightly in blues and greens. "I do believe her name is Liv, Bianca."

The other woman shook off this correction, looking at Adler for backup.

"Ms. Mantovani is correct," Adler stated matter-of-

CHAPTER SEVEN

"We don't need any more problems from you," Liv said under her breath, impersonating Adler Sinclair.

She hurried past the "Great Void," which was the name she was testing out for the strange blackness. Maybe the person she was on the hunt for right now would know what it was all about. Liv was in no hurry to start on the case she'd just been assigned. And besides, she had a standing date every evening that she wasn't about to miss. The brownies could wait.

Liv still couldn't believe that her next case involved intervening with the brownies about their work, imposing cleaning regulations on the small elves, who only wanted to serve by secretly cleaning the homes of mortals they admired.

Pulling open the large door to the residential area of the House of Seven, Liv stepped in carefully, checking behind the tapestry that hung on the closest wall. There was no one there.

She slid down the passageway, checking in a tall vase that stood next to a sideboard. Nothing.

Poking her head into the dining room, Liv ensured it was empty of people before entering. She browsed under the table, in the large cabinet at the back, and behind a large potted plant. Again she didn't find who she was looking for.

"Stay put, little monkey, because I will find you," Liv said in a whisper.

"You're talking to yourself again," Plato said. He had appeared suddenly at her side.

Liv shook her head. "You know damn well who I'm talking to."

"All I know is that you're not even close to finding her."

Liv regarded him with sudden curiosity. "Don't tell me. I want to do this on my own."

"I wouldn't dream of spoiling the fun."

Liv's eyes rose to the great chandelier that hung over the long table. Crystals of various colors dangled in strands from the tiers. Above the chandelier, the rafters of the ceiling seemed to go on forever. She used to think she saw little figures hiding there when she was a kid. She probably had, but the person she was looking for wouldn't be up there. At least, she hoped she wasn't, because then she wasn't going to be found.

"Liv?" a man called from the kitchen. "Are you looking for something to eat?"

She spun around to find Akio Takahashi. The Warrior had a sword sheathed at his side and wore long oriental silk robes. He was younger than his brother Haro by about a decade, but they shared the same boyish features.

"I'm not," Liv answered. "I'm looking for someone."

Akio stepped forward. In his hand, he held a large croissant. He eyed it for a moment, as if considering whether to eat it, then looked at Liv. "Can I help you?"

Liv shook her head. "It's sort of a game, and no offense, but you're not allowed to play."

He laughed, his brown eyes lighting up. "No offense taken. I'm not sure I have time for games anyway."

Liv couldn't stop herself from rolling her eyes. "Well, I guess I shouldn't either, but we must make time to play. And if I had more pressing cases, I might have less of a chance to play."

Akio took a bite of the croissant, his gaze thoughtful. "For a whole year, I was assigned to clean up after Lily Birds."

"'Lily Birds?'" Liv asked.

"Oh, they are a type of magical bird that crossed over from Europe long ago. They wreak havoc on this ecosystem if gone unchecked, but more importantly, they are quite hard to catch because they look like flowers."

Liv laughed. "Hence the name."

Akio nodded. "The work wasn't fun or exciting. It was quite tedious at times, and I feared I'd never find all of them and send them back to where they came from."

"But you did?"

"Yes, and then when the Councilors thought I was ready, they assigned me cases that I enjoyed more."

"Right, so the Council doesn't think I'm ready yet. I get it."

Akio tilted his head back and forth, considering the croissant. "That could very well be it. You are an unknown in the House. There are many questions about you."

An old memory rushed to the surface of Liv's mind. Not until she stared at the little boy in her memory did she remember something she wasn't sure how she had forgotten. "I grew up here with you. Do you remember that?"

"Yes, but I'm a bit older, which is why I'm surprised that you remember it."

The memory faded as she looked at the older Warrior. "But you left, didn't you?"

Akio nodded. "Our parents wanted Haro and me to spend our youth in Japan, knowing that one day we'd have to take our place here. But yes, I spent my formative years here before the age of twelve."

"Do you ever miss having that home away from this one?" Liv asked.

"I miss having an identity away from here," Akio said. "Our parents wanted us to have that, knowing that one day our obligation would be solely to the House of Seven. For ten years I was Akio Takahashi the magician, the schoolboy, the lover, the poet. Now I'm Akio the Warrior, and that is all."

Liv nodded. That made sense. How did people keep themselves from getting lost in this world? How would she? Then she reminded herself that this was only a twelve-year sentence. That was a long time, but it wasn't a lifetime. For a magician, that was less than ten percent of her allotted span. One day Sophia would replace Liv as Warrior, giving her a chance to take back her life.

"Your parents…" Liv trailed off, realizing that the question flirted with a sensitive topic.

meals. Liv had to duck several times as ingredients flew through the air, on course for a workstation. She hurried out into the gardens before the head chef sent a butcher knife in her direction. She'd noted the annoyed stare he'd given her as she traversed across the large kitchen.

The gardens had been one of Liv's favorite places growing up. When she stepped into the large yard surrounded by moss-covered walls, she felt part of her burden lift off her shoulders. Large topiaries of centaurs lined the path, their spears angled like arrows, pointing the way ahead.

Fountains ran the length of the garden. Crystal blue water sat as placid as glass, contrasting brilliantly with the green grass around the fountain. When Liv had been younger, she'd thought the ponds were shallow basins, until one day she had fallen in and found herself sinking so far down she nearly lost sight of the sunlight overhead. To this day, Liv couldn't remember how she made it out of the fountain, but it was too bizarre to have been a dream. All she recalled afterward was spitting up water for what felt like ages and receiving a stern lecture from her mother.

When she was confident there was no one hiding in the garden, Liv took the stairs to her favorite place in all of the House of Seven: the library.

There was no other place like it on Earth.

CHAPTER EIGHT

"Are you going to take Akio up on his offer?" Plato asked, materializing beside Liv as she topped the last set of stairs. The floor where the library was located held nothing else. That made sense, since the space was larger than all the residential rooms combined. One could spend months exploring the House of Seven's library and still not see it all. Liv knew that because she'd tried.

"You know, sometimes I think that you're a figment of my imagination," Liv said to the cat.

"Because I only talk to you?" Plato asked.

"And you disappear when others are around."

"I don't like people," he stated plainly.

"And I'm an exception?"

"You're a rarity."

"You like me," Liv sang in a teasing voice.

"I never said that."

"And I don't know about accepting training from Akio, although it could be a great opportunity."

"Your walls are crumbling," Plato observed.

Liv scoffed at him. "Maybe a little, but they are so tall that it will take eons for them to break down completely."

She pushed the thick door to the library open. Even though she was prepared for what she would see next, the place still filled her with awe. Columns as big as small cars rose all the way to the third-story ceiling overhead. Balconies were located in multiple places, each providing a view of the masterfully painted ceiling. A painting of the Milky Way Galaxy spiraled and sparkled, following the movements of the real galaxy.

The first floor of the library somehow felt quaint and cozy, with its multiple seating areas and reading nooks. However, Liv knew this was deceiving. Too many times she'd fallen asleep in one of the areas, only to wake in a place she didn't remember visiting. One didn't just get lost in this library. If you weren't careful, you became like a book passed along from reader to reader, shuffling through their shelves until at long last being found far from where you started.

Liv's mother had explained that when so many magical texts are kept in the same place, the books start to conspire against the readers, playing tricks on them.

When she reached the first row of books, Liv stopped, taking in a breath to welcome the scent of pages cloaked in dust and brimming with knowledge. She reached out and ran her fingers across the spines, enjoying the sensation as they tickled her skin.

When she was at the end of the row, Liv realized she was already lost. She turned in a complete circle, not knowing which way she'd come in. It suddenly felt like when she'd fallen into the fountain and didn't know which way was up and which way was down.

A giggle brought her back to the present, and Liv spun around. She caught a blur of blue to her right. Striding toward a large globe in a stand, she kept her eyes as unfocused as she could, knowing that was the best way to find the person she was looking for.

Another flash of blue, this time to the left. Liv halted. Waited. Listened for footsteps.

She heard them two rows over and doubled back that way.

"I know you're here," Liv whispered to the shelf of books.

Another giggle, this time closer.

Liv blinked, trying to will her eyes to relax and see the shelf of books as one rather than hundreds of separate volumes. It worked, and from the mix, a single book stood out. It was newer than all the rest. Brighter, its spine a sparkling blue.

Liv pointed at the book, muttering an incantation under her breath. The hardbound tome slipped off the shelf and hovered in the air before unfolding several times like a map, then all at once it blossomed into the form of Sophia Beaufont.

"I found you," Liv said nearly too loudly before catching herself.

Sophia beamed, displaying a row of bright teeth with one gap on the bottom. At age eight, she'd started to lose her teeth, but it didn't detract from the girl's exquisite beauty or her timeless appearance. She was every bit as complex as the thick volume on the history of magic she'd disguised herself as. Sophia Beaufont was a rare and extraordinary child.

She ran forward, wrapping her arms around Liv's waist. "I knew you would, although I got antsy during the long wait."

Liv gripped her back. "I can't believe you hid in a book."

Sophia stepped back and curtsied to Plato, who briefly acknowledged her. "Actually, to be exact, I disguised myself *as* a book."

"Well, I'm impressed."

Sophia held her finger to her lips. "This is still our secret? My use of magic?"

Liv nodded. "Of course. Just as our hide-and-seek game is."

Sophia smiled, her blue eyes twinkling. They matched the periwinkle dress she wore, which was full of ruffles and embroidered with yellow gems the color of her hair. "Good. I'll come up with an even better place tomorrow."

Sophia yawned, her mouth opening wide.

Liv reminded herself that this incredible magician was still a child. "Hey, it's your bedtime." She held out her hand. "Let's go," she said, more an order rather than a suggestion.

Sophia took her hand and allowed herself to be led away. Liv stopped, not entirely sure how to exit the library. "I forgot how to find my way out of this place."

The young magician chuckled, taking the lead. "It's like me when I want to be found. I gave you a clue, didn't I?"

"Oh, was *that* what all the giggling was about?" Liv teased.

"Yes, otherwise I would have been hiding forever,"

Sophia said, pointing up ahead to where a statue of a troll was indicating an open row.

"Was that there before?"

Sophia gave her a wink. "Probably not. The library changes based on what you want. If you want to leave, it points you in the right direction. If you want to hide, it gives you a place. And if you want to find out about smilgorms, it shoves you down that aisle."

"What are smilgorm?" Liv asked.

Sophia shook her head. "I don't know, and don't wonder about it, or we'll never make it out of here. Just focus on wanting the exit."

Liv did as she was told by her authoritative younger sister. One day she'd make an excellent Warrior, and until then, Liv would serve in her place, preserving the role for the Beaufont family.

CHAPTER NINE

The portal spat Liv out into an area of London that most mortals had never seen. Even if they saw it, they might not know what they were looking at. It actually took Liv several seconds to decipher the scene before her.

The cobblestone road was dark, although it was a strangely sunny day in London. The proximity of the buildings to the road made it so hardly any sunlight streaked down onto the pavement.

"Move to the side, sweetheart. Coming through," a man's voice said behind Liv. She jumped out of the way and turned to find a tall fae standing with his arms crossed. His maroon wings beat slightly as he regarded her with a mischievous smile. "Oh, it must be your first time on Roya Lane. You can't stand in the entrance, or no one can get through the portal. Newbie mistake."

"Roya Lane?" Liv asked, distracted by the sheer beauty of the man who stood before her. He had long ears like an elf, pointing out of his smooth blond hair, and he wore an elegant maroon tunic that matched his wings. An assortment of medals hung around his neck.

"Well, or as I like to call it, Government Center," he said, holding out a perfectly manicured hand to her. "My name is Rudolf. Who might you be, magician?"

Liv caught herself before blushing. She remembered then that the fae were deceptively beautiful. They'd made many a mortal fall in love with them over the centuries, leaving them lost and confused, pining for a lover who had long ago moved on.

She swallowed the tension in her throat and kept her face neutral, shaking Rudolf's hand. "I'm Liv Beaufont, a Warrior for the House of Seven."

Rudolf arched an eyebrow at her, his blue eyes smiling. "Do you have any identification? That's a big role for such a small girl to play."

Liv shook her head. "They don't issue us security badges at the House. Sorry."

Rudolf sighed, looking crestfallen. "Well, it appears I can't believe you then. My oath to the truth prevents me from taking others at their word. I always need proof."

"Umm, I'm not here to prove anything to you. I'm actually looking for the brownies' official office."

Raising his pointy chin high in the air, Rudolf turned his gaze to the blue sky. "I can't offer you any information since I don't know who you truly are."

Liv almost allowed a growl to escape her mouth. Who did this guy think he was, questioning her? "Yeah, that's not a problem. I'll just ask any of the other dozen creatures on Roya Lane." She turned her attention to the road, which was bustling with elves, gnomes, fairies of all sorts, and smaller creatures she could hardly make out that were streaking between the beings. The lane was closed off at the end; at Liv's back was a solid brick wall. The only way in was via portal-type magic, and apparently they were standing at that entrance since a group of elves nearly bowled them over as they entered the lane.

Rudolf grabbed Liv by the arm and pulled her to the side, out of the way. "You'll want to be careful to stay out of the portal area. And don't talk to McClusky. He'll steal your identity. And whatever you do, don't eat anything if it looks like it has peanuts. Firstly, it's probably not nuts, and secondly, it will make you break out in hives."

"Why are you helping me?" Liv asked, pulling her arm out of his grasp and nearly tripping on a small furry creature that scurried under their feet as it tried to get through the crowd. "I thought you refused to offer me any information since I couldn't prove my identity?"

"This is true, but I'm happy to offer a newbie to Roya Lane a small bit of knowledge so that you can navigate your way through the maze of this short road." Rudolf opened his arms wide, looking out over the street and smiling broadly.

"Great, so where is the brownies' headquarters?" Liv asked.

He shook his head. "I can't tell you that. What if you mean to kick down their door and assault them with your fists?"

Liv gave him an impatient stare. "That's not on my agenda, and all you'd be offering me is some directions. Not the code to a secret vault."

Rudolf laughed. "You are so new to this place. Without

directions to the brownies' office, you won't find it. I can assure you of that. Like brownies tend to be, it is hidden."

Liv looked down the row of doors, each one marked clearly: Gnome Headquarters, Elf Central, Fairy Affairs.

There were many other signs, but none of them said anything about Brownies.

"Look, Rudolf, what sort of proof of identity do you take? I have a driver's license and a lynx who can vouch for me."

Rudolf laughed. "Don't be absurd. A lynx wouldn't be allowed to enter this place. We have wards that prevent those pests from coming into Roya Lane."

"So you think," Liv muttered.

"Come again?"

Liv shook her head, dismissing him.

"And besides, I could no more accept the word of a lynx than that of a deranged jackrabbit. They each have their own agenda, and rarely is it to tell the truth."

"Right," Liv said, drawing out the word.

Rudolf looked Liv over, his eyes lingering a bit too long on her lower half. "Are you sure you don't have something on you that can tie you to the House of Seven? Maybe a shield with the Beaufont family crest?"

Liv opened her black cape. "Do you see a shield on me anywhere?"

Rudolf combed his hand over his chin. "I don't know. Maybe you should turn around."

Liv sighed; this conversation was going to kill all of her brain cells. Then a thought occurred to her and she pulled her mother's ring from her pocket, the one Ian had given to her. "I have this. Will that work?"

Rudolf's bright blue eyes widened when he saw the ornate ring with the center diamond and fourteen colorful gems around it. He reached out for it, but Liv pulled it back, giving him an untrusting look.

He dropped his hand and closed his gaping mouth. "Where are my manners? I apologize, Ms. Liv Beaufont. It's just that it has been so long since I've seen that ring. It took me back suddenly."

It was Liv's turn to gawk at him. "You've seen this ring before? On my mother, Guinevere Beaufont?"

Rudolf shook his head. "No, before her, but I honestly can't recall the memory. The harder I try, the more I seem to doubt it's my memory at all. Maybe it was your grand-mother who wore it, or your great grandmother, or the one before her." He shrugged, his face suddenly turning cheery. "Anyway, that's all the proof I need. I know that to be the Beaufonts' ring."

"You're very old, then?" Liv asked.

"Oh, the fae are the oldest of all magical creatures," Rudolf stated nobly. "We are older than the elves by at least a century." He cupped his mouth and leaned in Liv's direc-tion. "Don't try telling them that though. They'll get their tights in a wad."

"Well, maybe now you'll direct me to the brownies' headquarters," Liv said.

"I'll do you one better and escort you there myself, Liv Beaufont." He offered her his arm.

Liv considered taking it but decided it was better not to get too close to the fae. "Directions will do just fine."

Rudolf laughed, a soft melodic sound that made Liv's heart palpitate with sudden excitement. "You don't have to worry about me working my charms on you. It is I who should worry about falling for you, mademoiselle. A Warrior and a Beaufont. I dare say we would make beautiful children together and shake up the magical world at the same time. Oh, I do love a good scandal. Are you game?"

Liv lowered her chin and regarded him with a contemptuous glare. "Are you serious? Was that your attempt to ask me out?"

"That was my attempt to offer you the fruit of my loins and many years of intermittent bliss," Rudolf clarified, bowing to her.

"Yeah, I'm going to pass, but I still need to know where the brownies' headquarters is located."

"Very well, madam," Rudolf said, rising. "I see that you are a focused individual, and not to be distracted."

"The headquarters," Liv nearly barked.

"Follow me." Rudolf strode off through the crowd, cutting around a group of purplish creatures fighting over a potion bottle. "Do stay close. If I lose you, it might take one of your lifetimes to find me again, and by then I'll not want to gaze upon you because of your wrinkles."

"Wow, and you're single?" Liv asked in mock surprise. "I'm shocked."

"And here we are." Rudolf halted, gesturing at a plain brick wall.

"Is this one of those entrances that I can't see but you and the giants can?" she asked.

"No, I can't see the door either," Rudolf explained. "But I know it to be here."

"Your reasoning is flawed."

Rudolf laughed good-naturedly. "It's here, I assure you. Halfway between the Pegasus Corrections Facility and the Unclassified Magical Creatures Office."

"The what? No, that's not a thing."

"It is, though. There are still at least three dozen unclassified magical creatures. Well, that we know of."

"No, I meant...never mind," Liv said, waving him off as she studied Roya Lane. It was hard to believe there were so many different offices pertaining to magical creatures on this short, cramped street, and yet that was exactly how magic worked. It made the impossible possible.

"So this entrance? How am I supposed to get through it?" Liv asked, staring at the plain brick wall again.

"You simply declare who you are and state your business," Rudolf explained. "If you're granted access, the door will appear."

"Where can I get a door like this one?" Liv joked.

Rudolf apparently didn't think that was funny because he simply blinked at her dully.

"Oh, fine," she said, standing close to the wall. She felt like an idiot. "Liv Beaufont, Warrior of the House of Seven, is here to discuss cleaning regulations with the head brownie or brownie president or whatever your leader is called."

"Mortimer," Rudolf said.

"Huh?" Liv looked at him sideways.

"Mortimer is the Prime Minister of the brownies."

"Right," Liv said, turning back to the wall. "Liv Beaufont, Warrior of the House of Seven, here to see Mortimer."

"State your business," Rudolf cut in.

"So I can impose regulations set down by the Council of the House of Seven."

Nothing happened.

Liv's brow scrunched.

"It doesn't appear that Mortimer is willing to discuss such business today," Rudolf said, looking around. "Shall we go split a bottle of cherry wine and undress each other with our eyes?"

Liv ignored the fae and looked at the wall again. "Liv Beaufont, Warrior of the House of Seven, here to see Mortimer so that we can discuss the agreement between the brownies and the magicians."

Still no door appeared.

Liv looked at Rudolf and scowled. "If I find out that you have been joking with me by making me talk to a dumb wall, I'll mess up your hair and spread rumors that you're an awful kisser."

Rudolf gawked at her with disgust. "I have met some wicked Warriors in my time, but you, Liv Beaufont, are a new breed of evil."

She winked at him. "You have no idea." Turning back to the wall, she tried one more time. "Hey there, Mortimer. It's Liv Beaufont again. I was thinking that we could pretend to discuss boring House politics, but really I want to set up a mutual partnership. You know, an 'I scratch your back and you scratch mine' sort of thing?"

"Eww, you do realize that brownies are awfully hairy and probably never wash their backsides properly? Now my back, you're welcome to scratch and rub for hours," Rudolf offered.

"It's an expression," Liv told him. "And I'd rather take a bath with a gnome than touch your unclothed body."

"Methinks that implies you'd like to touch my clothed body." Rudolf gave her a wolfish grin. "I get that you must take things slowly, but I beseech you to not waste too much time since you have only a few hundred years left compared to me."

Liv rolled her eyes, turning back to the brick wall. She was about to give up when an arched door only three feet tall appeared.

"Well, it looks like they've accepted the invitation you've thrust upon them," Rudolf said.

CHAPTER TEN

"How am I supposed to fit through that door?" Liv asked, pointing.

"Your hips are a bit meaty, but I think we can wedge you through the doorway," Rudolf said, holding out his hands. "I'll push from the rear end."

Liv held up a finger. "If you so much as look at my ass, I'll break that little button nose of yours."

Rudolf cupped his hands over his nose. "So many threats. What makes you so hostile, my lady?"

"Jerks with big wings and small—"

"Do not finish that sentence," he said, cutting her off as he clapped his hands to his ears.

Liv shook him off and turned her attention to the small door. She could fit through it, but she wasn't going to look graceful doing it. Turning the handle, she pushed it open and peered through. A long, nondescript hallway led to a door at the end. The paint on the walls was peeling, and the area smelled like an old lunchbox.

"I'm going in," Liv said, pulling her head back out of the door.

"Let me know if you want a push," Rudolf said, holding out his hands.

"Let me know if you want a black eye," she sang back.

He laughed as she put her head through the door and worked to crawl through. "You are quite delightful with your jokes, Liv Beaufont. We should have a drink sometime."

"Yeah, yeah," Liv called back dismissively.

"Until we meet again."

"Hopefully later rather than sooner," she said, edging forward on her elbows and knees. There was a tacky substance on the floor inside the headquarters and she stuck to the dirty tile. Once she was through the door, it closed automatically, leaving her alone to look down the short hallway.

The sconces on the walls flickered like the bulbs were going bad and a loud banging sound radiated from the far end of the corridor.

Liv tried to stand but had to stay hunched so as not to hit her head on the ceiling, which was covered in spider webs. Brownies might take it upon themselves to clean the houses of mortals they admired, but ironically, they didn't appear to keep their own place very tidy.

When she'd come to the door on the far end, Liv knocked. The banging stopped.

"Come in," a squeaky voice called.

Liv opened the door and peered through to find a small, cramped office piled high with books and papers. They covered the desk on the opposite side of the room

Mortimer shot her a look of disbelief. "You can't be serious? One of *my* brownies?"

"Well, their job *is* to clean, and I just thought—"

"Our job *isn't* to clean." Mortimer stood, his height not changing at all. "That is our passion. We do it out of love. Out of loyalty. It is my job to assign work and monitor it, and intervene when necessary, but cleaning is not part of a job. And how could I ask one of my loyal subjects to spend their energy on me when it isn't me they worship, but rather the noble mortals who slave away all day at thankless jobs and drag themselves home to bed, usually too tired to clean the sink full of dishes. Oh, no, this is my mess, and therefore my responsibility. But alas, I'm too busy to do the job."

Yeah, too busy, Liv thought, eyeing the ball sitting on his desk.

"Well, *my* house could use some help," Liv stated. "Maybe a brownie will worship me."

"You aren't a mortal. Magicians don't need our help because they can rely on their magic," Mortimer said. "But your friend John is a nice fellow." He picked up a piece of paper from the mess and read it silently for a second. "A noble fellow with strong moral convictions. Hard-working. Kind. Good to his employees."

"Employee," Liv corrected, surprised that Mortimer could find nothing in the office but had pulled that report straight from the desk.

"And he pets his dog first thing upon entering his dwelling," Mortimer continued, reading from the paper.

"So John gets his house cleaned?" Liv asked. "I guess that's at least something."

"Well, I'm deciding whether his shop should be included. He has a brownie who is quite taken with him and would like to extend his services to include more."

"Just as long as they don't reorganize my tools," Liv stated. "I have a system."

"So, you, Liv Beaufont, Warrior of the House of Seven, aren't here to force more rules upon me?"

Liv thought for a moment and then shrugged. "Let's say I did and then I won't."

"What if your Council were to find out about this?"

"I'm pretty certain they just gave me the case to keep me out of their hair, but let's pretend that you agreed. Once I leave here, you can operate as you were, and I'll act the fool if they confront me about it."

Mortimer took a seat again in his chair. "I've never met a Warrior such as yourself. You don't seem to have any loyalty to the House."

"Oh, I do. I just don't see the point in useless regulations. Why is it our business how you do your job…I mean, fulfill your passion?"

"So how may I scratch your back, then?"

"There are a couple of things, actually," Liv began, formulating different ideas in her head. "Brownies are in a position to see and hear a lot, correct?"

"Oh, yes. We are always in the shadows, unseen."

"I thought so," Liv said triumphantly. "I was hoping that you could spread the word to your brownies to have them watch out for a canister of magic."

"Canister of magic, you say?"

"Yes. It went missing recently, and I'm not sure where it was sent."

"And why do you think that it would be in a mortal's possession?" Mortimer asked.

"I don't," Liv answered. "That's just the thing. I have no idea where it might be. However, it can't hurt to have your people keeping an eye out."

"And in return, you will leave us alone and allow us to operate as we have?"

"Well, I might also have a few more favors to ask of you," Liv hedged.

"Like what?" Mortimer snapped a piece of the brittle off and took a bite.

"Well, for instance, do you know why magic would be protecting a giant's sword in a mortal-run museum?" Liv asked, deciding she had better trust Mortimer if she wanted more information. Even if he told anyone about her questions, she wasn't sure what harm it would do. She was simply investigating.

"Mortals don't have magic," Mortimer finally stated after taking a long moment to chew. "It must have been magicians who put the wards on the sword."

"That was my thought," Liv said. "I just don't understand why."

Mortimer took another bite of the brittle, looking thoughtful. "I think there is much about this situation that you don't understand. I'll have my brownies keep out an eye for the canister and information on the sword and think more about it. Will that suffice for our agreement? It is getting on to nap time."

Liv nodded, standing and hitting her head on the low ceiling. "Yes. I'll be in touch with you to see if you find any information."

Mortimer picked a piece of candy out of his yellow teeth. "No, it is we who will notify you."

"How?" Liv asked.

"We brownies have our ways. Look for a message from us."

CHAPTER ELEVEN

Everyone in the damn magical world was trying to make Liv crazy. Gone were the days where things were normal and she could look around John's shop without constant paranoia. Since talking to Mortimer, she constantly looked around for a sign from the brownies that they'd found something or had information for her. A rolled-up candy wrapper sitting in a place she hadn't remembered seeing one became cause to pace back and forth for an hour, wondering if she should revisit Roya Lane to speak with the Prime Minister of the brownies.

"I wonder if you're being overly sensitive and over-thinking the whole thing," Plato said, stretching out on the workbench and rolling over to expose his belly.

"You think?" Liv replied, fidgeting with a computer monitor's wires. She couldn't figure out exactly what the problem was yet, even though she'd been studying it for the better part of an hour.

She was so engrossed in her work that she didn't even

look up when the door chimed, signaling that someone had entered.

"What are you doing?" Clark asked.

Liv looked up to find her brother with his hands pressed to his pinstriped slacks, his dragonhide cloak covering his shoulders.

"A better question is, what are you wearing?" Liv asked.

Clark looked down at his three-piece suit. "What do you mean?"

Liv waved her hand at him, the one with a small screwdriver in it. "You're dressed like you're going to the theater…in 1890."

"Ha-ha," Clark said with no inflection in his voice. "This is a perfectly decent way to dress in this day and age."

"How many strange looks did you get on the street?" Liv asked.

"Mortals always look at me strangely," Clark answered. "It's because they are enamored of my regal appearance."

"Yep, that's it."

Clark strode forward, careful to not brush against anything, that might damage his pressed suit. "What are you doing?"

Liv looked down at the monitor. "I'm trying to fix this hunk of junk."

"Well, why don't you use…" Clark looked around. "Well, you know."

Liv nodded. "I've done that before. It doesn't turn out well unless I know exactly what's wrong with the device, so I'm trying to figure it out."

Clark looked around at the shop. On the far wall, John had a collection of old cameras, ones that dated back to before the turn of the last century. "I'm still at a loss for why you work. The House has started to pay you, right?"

"Yes, but doing a job is sometimes less about getting paid and more about fulfilling a responsibility."

A smile surfaced on Clark's face. "You sound like Dad."

Liv bristled and opened her mouth to say something sarcastic, but nothing came to mind. Finally, she said, "Yeah, well, he was right when he said things like that. Actually, he was always right."

Clark sighed. "You thought too highly of them."

"How is that even possible? They were our parents."

"Well, you can't even consider that their deaths were an accident because you don't see them as ever making a mistake. I'm not saying you're wrong, not after what we've recently learned about the canister of magic, but you've got to have some objectivity."

"Point to one person in the world who sees their parents objectively," Liv demanded, thrusting the screwdriver into the screw's slot with a bit more force than she intended. "From the beginning, they keep us alive. Through acts of selflessness and sacrifice, they teach us about love, and from our earliest memories, they are our heroes, saving us from the dark or a bad dream. Who are these people who look at their parents and see them as anything but extraordinary? Because if they have parents like ours and don't revere them, there is something seriously wrong with them."

Clark dared to flash Liv a rebellious smile. It made his usually conservative face look roguish. "For someone who likes to pretend she doesn't care about family, I think you're the most loyal of us all."

Liv picked the screwdriver back up. "I am not."

"You are too."

"I am...not playing this game with you."

Clark started pacing around the shop, looking the various devices over but never touching any of them. "So the canister... I keep trying to discreetly check for leads, but I haven't found anything yet."

Liv nodded, glad to have the subject changed. "Yeah, me too."

"I also keep mulling over Reese's words. Have you been able to make sense of them?" he asked.

Liv looked up absentmindedly, the words falling out of her mouth, rehearsed: *"Olivia has the key. You have the heart. Together you must finish what we started."*

"Reese was always the poet and creative one, wasn't she?" Clark said, fondness in his voice.

"Yes, but it wouldn't have killed her to be literal this one time," Liv said, and immediately regretted her choice of words. Clark's face turned grave as he busied himself looking at an old rotary phone.

"I don't get how I could have the key," Liv said in a rush to cover her blunder. "And if anyone has less heart then it's you."

Clark shot her a punishing look over the shelf. "Hey, I've been working to keep the Councilors off your back. If it weren't for me, those sessions at the House might be worse. They disapprove of your tactics, like how you handled the goblins, but I got them to see some of the good that might come out of shaking up our allies and making them realize who is in control."

Liv shook her head. "It shouldn't be about bullying.

That's the problem. The House has all these exceptions for goblins and gnomes or whatever. There is no fairness or balance. We're supposed to serve justice, but all we do is enforce a bunch of arbitrary laws that we set up."

"I've heard this speech of yours before," Clark said, striding around the shelf and eyeing Plato, who was pretending to sleep beside Liv.

She tensed when the door at the back of the shop opened. That sound didn't usually bring such a reaction, but she wasn't usually in the presence of another magician. She looked around quickly as if trying to find a hiding place to stash Clark.

Pickles bolted through the open door to the back, running straight up to Clark and jumping on his leg, leaving behind dirty paw prints.

Her brother shooed the dog off, giving Liv an annoyed glare as he wiped his pants.

Any hope Liv had of getting her brother out of there unseen evaporated when John sauntered through the door, pausing at the sight of Clark. "Well, hello there, neighbor. Is Liv taking care of you?"

"Neighbor?" Clark asked, confused. "I actually don't live in the neighborhood, and I was only coming by to—"

"This is my brother," Liv said in a rush, surprising herself with her honesty. *See, telling the truth wasn't so hard.* She'd just done it. "And he's dressed like that because he's an actor." Her face filled with heat at the horrified expression Clark gave her. *Okay, honesty was a process.* She'd get there.

"B-b-brother?" John asked, looking between Liv and Clark. "You never mentioned having a brother."

Clark shot her an expression that seemed to say, "shocking."

"Yeah, he's been away," Liv said. "Traveling with his acting troupe."

"Troupe?" Clark mouthed when John put his back to him.

She blushed.

"Oh, well, that's exciting." John offered Clark his hand, shaking the magician's warmly. "Nice to meet you…"

"Clark," her brother supplied.

"Nice to meet you, Clark," John offered. "Any family of Liv's is welcome here. Are you going to be staying with her?"

"Here?" Clark asked with disbelief, nearly laughing before covering his expression, urged by the look on Liv's face. "And ummm, no. I live in Santa Monica. I was just stopping by to pay her a visit."

"Oh, well, that's sure nice of you," John said, looking between Liv and Clark. "I bet it will be nice to catch up. There's nothing quite like having family close by."

"But not too close," Liv said, chancing a rude glare at Clark when John wasn't looking.

"Yes, I'll try to stop by for lunch when I'm in the neighborhood," Clark said.

"Sometimes I'm too busy to eat," Liv stated.

John puffed out his cheeks and shook his head. "Now that's nonsense, Liv. You've got to eat, and you've earned those lunch breaks. I daresay you don't take as many breaks as you should. If a human resources representative came into the shop, they might cite me for being in violation of some people code."

"There's no such thing, John," Liv said with a laugh, trying to change the subject. She didn't know how she felt about her old world and her new world colliding like this. She was trying to protect John by not telling him about magic, but if her brother showed up regularly, it would become increasingly difficult. Clark didn't look like a hipster hanging out in North Hollywood. With his chiseled face and strange clothes, he most assuredly looked like a magician, but she hoped that John wouldn't figure that out.

"Well, I'll leave you two to catch up," John said, picking up Pickles and letting the dog lick his face. "I'll be back this evening to help you close up, Liv."

"Thanks," she sang as the old man and the dog exited through the front.

"So, your boss doesn't know a thing, does he?" Clark asked when they were alone again.

"I've heard it's better that way," Liv explained.

Clark nodded. "You'd be putting him in danger if he knew the truth about you. You might not yet, but soon you'll have enemies. Every Warrior has them. It goes with the territory."

Liv's insides cramped. The idea of putting John and the shop in danger was a new stress she didn't know how to deal with yet.

Reading the tension on her face, Clark said, "You could always move into the House of Seven. It's safe there. You wouldn't have to worry about any of this then. You wouldn't have to worry about working here."

Liv sighed. "I don't worry about working. It's what keeps me sane when the House of Seven is driving me crazy. But I don't want anything to happen to John."

"Well, then you're going to have to be careful going forward," Clark warned. "It's only a matter of time before you piss off someone in the magical community and they come after you. If they can't find you, they usually go after those you love."

Liv nearly bolted out of her seat, her emotions making her insides hop around. "This pep talk has been delightful. You're a real ray of sunshine, brother. Let's do this again soon, and by soon, I mean never again. I'll come to you. Don't come here."

Clark regarded her dully for a long moment. "Okay, fine. But I'm here if you need help with any of this...mortal stuff."

Liv wasn't sure if she believed Clark, but he seemed sincere.

He rolled his shoulders, trying to release some tension. "Look, about the other stuff... I'm going to try to get closer to Adler and figure out if he's involved in this canister business. Everything I've gathered so far suggests that he is."

"So I shouldn't be offended if you blow me off when I'm at the House of Seven, then?"

"You know that we have to play things carefully," Clark said. "It's better if it doesn't look like we're working together, or someone might get suspicious."

"Well, what am I supposed to do in the meantime, while you're stomaching the presence of that evil albino who lives to humiliate me in front of the others?"

"Work on figuring out what Reese was talking about," Clark suggested. "If she says you have the key, figure out what that is and how to use it."

He plucked up another kitten and popped the bottle into its mouth. "No, giants don't mess with potions."

Liv lifted Junebug, eyeing the furball as he wiggled. "Well, then I'm going to conclude that you're doing a noble deed, caring for kittens in the absence of their mother. That's really wonderful of you."

Rory scowled at her. "Actually, yes. I plan on eating the kittens. Giants' favorite snacks are puppies and kittens."

Liv set Junebug down and removed the solid-orange kitten who was curled up inside Rory's boot. "I don't know, Samson. I think the giant is fibbing, but I'm onto his game. He's a do-gooder."

"I am not," Rory answered, narrowing his eyes as Junebug made the climb up the coffee table again. "And the kittens don't understand English. Believe me, I've tried."

Liv reached over and grabbed the daredevil kitten, holding him in one hand and Samson in the other. "No wonder Plato didn't want to come in here. It's cuteness overload."

Rory set down the kitten he was feeding. "The lynx didn't want to come in here because he's intimidated."

A laugh burst out of Liv's mouth, scaring Samson. "Plato, intimidated? That would be a first. Why would a bunch of rambunctious kittens intimidate Plato?"

"Because they are their authentic selves," Rory answered. "What you see is what you get, but the lynx can't say the same thing. He is always deceiving people in one way or another."

Liv felt like that was a personal insult to her, but she shook it off, realizing that Rory was partly right. Plato was a mystery, but that didn't mean he was untrustworthy.

"Hey, I was wondering about this long-standing feud between the giants and the magicians," Liv said, thinking about what the Council had said regarding giants. "What caused the rift?"

Rory stood, slipping one of the kittens into the breast pocket of his shirt.

Liv pointed to the squirming little animal and laughed. "Snack for later?"

He nodded, not looking at all amused. "Have you read the book I gave you?"

"Parts of it," she said, trying to remember the last time she'd had time to crack open *Mysterious Creatures* by Bermuda Laurens.

"The book is over a thousand pages long," Rory said with stern disappointment. "If you've only read parts, you're missing a great deal."

"That book isn't that long," Liv argued. "It's not thick enough to be."

Rory shook his head and trudged toward the backyard, many of the kittens attacking his bare feet as he did. "When are you going to learn that nothing is what it seems with magic? The book is enchanted to fit in your pocket or not take up much room on a shelf."

Liv followed him out. "Wait, I thought that giants don't believe in using glamour to make their houses or whatever look different than they are?"

Rory stopped abruptly, his hand out to the side to halt Liv. He turned slowly. "We like things to appear as they are, but we're also about efficiency. If that means making a book more compact, that's fine."

"Well, you should have used that spell on yourself so you could have gotten into that SUV the other day."

With his hand still out, Rory said, "It's time for you to leave."

"But I just got here," Liv argued. "Aren't you going to train me?"

He shook his head. "Go home and read the book."

She tried to look around the giant, but he moved so he was firmly blocking the door.

"I'm working on your sword, and I can't share the secrets of the metalworking process that were passed to me by my grandfather," Rory explained.

"Do the kittens get to see?" Liv asked, watching as one of them climbed up Rory's leg.

"Any luck with getting to Turbinger?" Rory asked, referring to his grandfather's sword.

Liv deflated slightly. "No, not yet. I've been asking around, but I haven't found out anything that will help me get closer."

"Might I suggest that you simply try to get closer and find out exactly what obstacles await you?"

Liv lowered her chin and regarded him from hooded eyes. "That sounds like a recipe for disaster. Are you going to bail me out if I get thrown in jail?"

Rory turned and trudged out the door. "Nope. You're a magician. I expect you to figure out how to get yourself out."

CHAPTER THIRTEEN

Before Liv had magic, breaking into a museum to steal a sword as tall as she was would have sounded impossible. However, with magic, many things seemed doable. Rory couldn't get to the sword for whatever reason, but that shouldn't mean that Liv couldn't.

She breezed past tourists looking at ancient artifacts, head down and eyes scanning her surroundings. Once again, the room with Turbinger was empty when she came to it. Stopping at the entry, Liv looked around. There was nothing besides the sword in the area, which was weird, because all the other rooms she'd passed had held statues or the remains of prehistoric animals or humans.

Liv took a step into the room, and for a moment she felt as if something wrapped around her. A forcefield? She dismissed this idea, thinking her imagination was getting the better of her.

She was accosted by the sword's sheer beauty once she stood in front of it. Before, she'd been so distracted by Rory and his mysterious nature that she'd been unable to fully appreciate the craftsmanship. It was obvious to her that the sword held a great deal of magic, but she wasn't sure why she was positive about that.

Holding her hands a few inches from the glass, Liv began to mutter different incantations, ones she'd only learned an hour ago. When Rory had told her to read the book he'd given her, she'd gone home and opened it randomly, surprised to find hundreds of pages devoted to magicians' spellwork. That seemed strange to her since she had thought the book provided information on other species like gnomes and trolls and whatever else. The more Liv flipped through the book, the more she realized that it was a vast encyclopedia of information on all things magical. That was when she glanced at the cover and something sunk in: *she* was a mysterious creature. All her life, she'd thought of other magical species as "creatures" and her own as "magicians." People who had powers. But they were all creatures full of mystery and magic.

Not only had Liv not expected to learn much about her kind in a book written by a giant, but she was surprised to find incantations that rolled off her tongue more fluidly than ones she'd learned years ago in the House of Seven. The incantations written by Bermuda Laurens were clean and easy to speak, sounding natural to Liv.

Her fingers tingled as the first incantation rolled out of her mouth, and for a few seconds, Liv expected for the case to open and the sword to rise into the air. When it didn't, she tried a second incantation, and then a third. All of them were about opening up or breaking into locked objects.

Liv let her fingers drop to the glass case and immediately felt a shock ripple through her hands. She jumped back, eyeing the case with irritation as the jolts continued to pour through her arms and up her shoulders.

"Miss, is everything alright?" a voice called from behind her.

Liv spun around to find a security guard peeking into the room.

"It's fine," Liv said, dropping her still-aching arms to her sides.

The guard looked at her and the sword display, uncertainty written on his face. Dismissing his concerns, he strode over, his attention fully on the sword.

"It's quite the beauty, isn't it?" he asked, stepping up next to her.

"Yeah. It's unlike anything I've ever seen," Liv stated.

He nodded. "Apparently, you're not the only one, since they don't know much about the object." The guard pointed to the placard beside the sword, which had little information on it.

"I wonder how much it weighs?" Liv mused aloud, mostly to herself.

"That's a good question," the guard stated.

"Does it take multiple people to lift it when they open the case?" Liv asked.

The guard's face scrunched in confusion. "Open the case? I've never seen them do that."

"Oh, but surely they have to at some point."

He shrugged. "I'm not sure why they would. There's really no reason to."

"What about for cleaning or maintenance?" Liv didn't know where her questions were going, but she hoped that something she could use would come out of them.

"Nah, that glass is sealed so that no air can get in and nothing can get out." The guard knocked on the surface of the case and smiled. "It's impenetrable."

Liv expected the guard to retract from a shock, and when he didn't, she kept her face neutral with an effort. "Yes, it seems as though it's quite strong."

"Well, when you're done here," the guard pointed over his shoulder, "you should check out the mummies in the next room over. They are quite creepy."

Liv waved, subtly dismissing the man. "I'll definitely do that. Thanks."

After he was gone, Liv extended her hand again, letting it hover an inch above the glass. Maybe the shock she had received before had just been a result of too much built-up static electricity. Maybe it had been the incantations trying to work. She couldn't be sure what had caused it, but she didn't think it would happen twice.

Allowing her hand to drop, her fingertips had been in contact with the case for less than a second when a mind-numbing shock knocked her back several feet. Liv landed on her backside and slammed against the wall. The incident set off the alarms, making red lights strobe overhead. The sirens blared, seeking to wake Liv up from the daze the electric shock had sent through her body. She tried to stand, but her limbs were uncooperative.

"Hey! What's going on in here?" the guard yelled, sprinting back into the room. He looked at Liv, crouched on the ground, and then the case. "Did you try to open it? What did you do?"

"I didn't do anything," Liv argued, sweat beading her forehead as she tried again to get to her feet. The effort was almost too much, making her think that she'd tumble over on her side.

"Keep your hands where I can see them," the guard yelled, his eyes anxiously bouncing between Liv and the case. He pulled out a gun and pointed it at Liv when she finally made it to a standing position.

Oh no, that won't do, Liv thought, looking at the nervous guard.

"Just stay where you are until backup arrives," he ordered, the hand holding his gun shaking.

Blood dripped from Liv's nose. She wiped it away with her hand, realizing she must look like quite the sight to the mortal before her.

Running footsteps echoed in the corridor behind her; she had to get out of there. But she felt too weak to run, much less use magic.

"I must have passed out and fallen on the case," Liv explained, rolling back her shoulders and trying to summon new strength. She remembered something she'd read in Bermuda's book that morning about pulling from the elements. That was how giants' magic worked. She began to siphon energy, but she wasn't sure where it was coming from. All she knew was that a moment later she felt a great flood of magical energy pouring through her. Then she reminded herself that she was in the Natural History Museum, where there was probably ancient sources of elemental energy to draw from.

The guard looked at her with uncertainty. "You fell on the case? That was what caused the alarms?"

"I think so," Liv said, testing her balance. She was feeling steadier with every passing second.

"That doesn't make any sense. We'll have to check the cameras," the guard said, indicating the cameras in the corner.

Oh hell, Liv thought. She had to do more than just get away now.

The footsteps were getting closer.

As quickly as she could manage, which was much faster than anything she'd ever done before, Liv directed her hand at the camera. It exploded, sending sparks and bits of debris out from the corner. She hoped that it erased the feed, which was something she'd been practicing in her spare time at the shop.

Liv shielded her head and spun around, her arm coming down over the guard's before he realized what was happening. The gun clattered to the ground as she sent her other arm into his midsection, making him double over. The movements weren't graceful, but they got the job done.

Knowing that she was seconds away from being trapped, Liv ran for the exit. Making a portal wouldn't work. She hadn't been able to use portal magic to get into the museum, which meant she couldn't use it to get out of there.

Three guards with their guns by their sides were hurrying in her direction.

"Stop!" the front one yelled.

That was not going to happen, Liv thought, holding up her hand and sending a blast of arctic wind in their direction, which knocked them back several feet. She still wished she had learned fireball magic, but the wind got the job done.

The sirens overhead were still blaring and many

patrons had peeked their heads out of the various rooms, their curious eyes on Liv.

Several were holding up phones, recording her every move. Directing her hand at them, she disabled the phones, deleting the footage. *She needed to get out of there.*

More guards were on the way; she knew that since the civilians were looking over their shoulders toward the main entrance. *So not that way,* Liv thought, making a split-second decision and barreling in the opposite direction.

Liv needed a diversion. A way to hold the guards off. The dinosaur bones in the distant atrium caught her eyes. She lifted her hand to bring the bones down in a heap of destruction but hesitated. The only way she could destroy goblins homes was if she knew she was going to put them back together, and the same went for prehistoric dinosaurs.

No, Liv was better than that—or at least she wanted to be.

"Hey, free money!" she yelled, throwing both her hands in the air and muttering an incantation which she knew to be purely a party trick, one she'd seen many in the House of Seven use at parties when she was a child.

From the tall ceiling, crisp dollar bills floated down. The crowd streamed out of their hiding places, most abandoning recording their videos to dash out and snatch up the money before others could get to it.

Liv sprinted down the corridors to the stairs, knowing that was her only hope of getting out of there. She glanced over her shoulder before taking the stairs to the second level. The crowd had spread out, creating a wall impossible for the guards to get around. Not only that, but there would be mass confusion for a while. The museum might not even know exactly what the real disturbance had been since the camera in the giant's sword room had been destroyed and its footage.

That reminded Liv of something, and when she came to the second level, she pointed to the first floor, making all of the security cameras explode, erasing the recording. Mortals screamed from the disturbance, but their cries were drowned out by laughter and excitement as they shoved dollar bills into their pockets—money that would disappear within the hour.

Liv knew that her options on the second floor were limited. She had to get out of the building. From all directions she heard yelling and stomping as the guards closed in on her, so she made an impromptu decision and thrust her hand in the direction of a bank of tall windows. They all exploded in a cacophony of noise. Liv ducked until the glass shards had settled on the tile floor, then dashed for the windows and jumped through, landing on a nearby roof.

The guards had made it to the second level and were shouting, their guns drawn as they ran over to the shattered windows.

Liv took off, sprinting across the top of the building, realizing that soon she was going to have to climb up higher or jump down lower. Taking the less intimidating option, she rebounded off the roof and caught the edge of the building, but only barely. Her legs dangled down, banging against the brick. Trying to keep her momentum, Liv kicked her legs over the side and managed to pull herself up, like she used to climb out of the pool not using the ladder.

Liv was giving herself a moment to feel victorious when she heard the whirring of the blades of a helicopter barreling in her direction. There was shouting behind her, and then gunfire. She was suddenly a fugitive. A criminal, the thing she fought against. And then she remembered who she was: a magician.

Liv dashed forward, putting as much space as she could between her and the forces at her back. When she came to the end of that building, she leapt down to the building below and ran across an orange rooftop. She didn't know the layout of the building, but glancing up ahead, she saw that the roof came to an abrupt end. However, she had to be careful with her exit or hundreds of mortals would see her getting away. That would be very bad for business.

When she was almost at the end of the roof, Liv changed directions and jumped down to the roof below. The drop was farther than she had anticipated, and she had to roll to displace her momentum. The drop to the next level wasn't as far.

She could see that guards had already lined up on the ground, facing the building with their guns at the ready. That was fine, because she needed a well-placed distraction. She sent a projection of a figure that looked a lot like her but also not at all, leaping over the edge of the roof to the lawn below. At the exact same time, Liv opened a portal on the rooftop and jumped through, closing it as quickly as she could. She tumbled through it, landing on the boardwalk in Santa Monica in an exhausted heap, grateful to be far from the mayhem that she'd created.

CHAPTER FOURTEEN

"Do you think anyone saw all that?" Liv asked Plato as she brushed off her clothes and strode down the long corridor to the Chamber of the Tree.

"Just a horde of Asian tourists," Plato answered. "But they are probably still busy trying to stuff dollar bills into their pockets."

"Do you think that last trick distracted them enough?"

Plato yawned. "I'm not sure. Time will tell."

"Hey, and you're allergic to kittens?" she asked, remembering what Rory had said. "What's up with that?"

A visible shiver ran down Plato's back. "They are deceptively cute."

"So it's not for some other reason?"

"I'll be the first to admit that I have certain flaws in my makeup. They don't always make sense, but we all have them."

"I think we should discuss this further later," Liv said, halting in front of the Door of Reflection. "For now, I'm going to go tell the Council what they want to hear."

"And the rumor is that *I'm* the deceptive one," Plato grumbled, a hint of playfulness in his voice.

"I think you're misunderstood," Liv replied as she took a step forward.

"Oh, and Liv?" Plato called at her back. "The proximity of the white tiger or the black crow to you is important. Pay attention to that."

"Important how?" Liv asked. "I thought you said you didn't know anything about them."

"I didn't, but much like you, I pick up new information all the time." Plato nodded to the wall. "Go in there now while the Council is distracted."

Adler looked to be visibly shaking when Liv entered the chamber. "And you took it upon yourself to intervene?"

Trudy DeVries lifted her chin and blinked several times. The white tiger stood only a few feet away from her, its unwavering attention on the Warrior. "The situation wasn't out of my control, although it was clear that it would soon escalate if I didn't do something."

Adler pressed his knobby fingertip into his temple. "Do you recognize the trouble you've made for the House with your actions?"

"Sir, if I may," Stefan stepped off his circle on the ground and moved forward as Liv took her place.

"You may not," Adler said harshly, his eyes flicking to Liv briefly. "Ms. DeVries has brought much scrutiny on the House by sympathizing with a nonregistered magician in public."

accidentally set off an alarm in a bank vault at one of the major branches of a bank downtown. SWAT forces were called, and you had to do quite a lot of magic in order to keep from being apprehended."

Raina joined in. "I heard about that, although it was before my time." She looked down the bench at Adler. "Didn't you overturn several vehicles trying to flee? The news didn't know what to make of it. They called it the strangest heist in history since nothing was stolen and no one was apprehended."

Liv did not remember ever seeing Adler so angry, his usually pale face currently a dark scarlet. "I don't think that past incident has any bearing on what Ms. Beaufont has done."

"I think it does," Haro cut in, his tone musing. "It proves that sometimes magicians can be caught in circumstances beyond their control. We control our magic, and yet we can't control how it affects certain systems. For instance, your magic set off security systems that guarded against magical thievery."

Mortal security systems that guarded against magic? Liv had never heard of such a thing. Before she could roll the questions around in her head anymore, the Councilors erupted in a barrage of arguing. Adler spun back and forth to combat what Haro, Raina, and Hester were saying.

"Look what you've done," Stefan said from the corner of his mouth.

"Me?" Liv mouthed in return. "I was just in the wrong place at the wrong time."

"Right. What was this case you touched?"

She shrugged. "I think it was dinosaur teeth or something."

"Hmmm," Stefan said, a slight smile on his face.

"The past is inconsequential!" Adler yelled, making the entire chamber go silent. His breath rattled between his lips several times as he regained his composure. "We must be careful with the disturbances we create."

"I'm sorry," Liv said honestly. "I didn't mean to cause any trouble. And once things got out of hand, I tried to minimize the damage and get away without being seen."

Looking up from her screen, Hester nodded. "It appears you were successful. The authorities have no leads on the suspect who got away and are calling the entire incident a mystery. It seems that once again, magicians have simply been the victim of technology." She smiled thoughtfully at Liv. "This happens more than most realize. It wasn't your fault."

Liv swallowed and tried to nod.

"Still, in the future, don't put yourself in situations that you know could put us all under scrutiny," Adler warned.

"He means, stay away from bank vaults and museums," Raina clarified with a laugh.

"I meant that you should spend less time galivanting around and more time working on cases and training," Adler said impatiently. "Another case has been sent to your device, Ms. Beaufont."

Liv lifted her tablet and read the first line from the new case. She expected it to say something like Wipe Fairies' Asses.

She laughed to herself when she read the case file.

"Is everything all right, Olivia?" Bianca asked, having read the sour expression on her face.

"Oh, this is fine," Liv stated. "Just starting to feel clairvoyant. And again, for the hundredth time, my name is Liv."

Adler rolled his eyes. "There has been no sign of clairvoyance in the Beaufont family to date."

"No, I just meant that I was certain I'd get a case of this sort," Liv stated, and then something occurred to her. "Actually, my magic... Has it normalized yet, or is it still showing a spike since being unlocked?"

Adler sighed as if he were bored with the whole conversation suddenly. "It's really no concern of yours."

"It's *my* magic!" Liv found herself yelling.

Hester smiled good-naturedly down at Liv. "It's still showing a bit high, my dear, but it's nothing to worry about."

"I would disagree," Haro cut in. "Liv blew out multiple windows in the Natural History Museum and created a projection of herself while simultaneously creating a portal. That kind of magic is unprecedented for a magician with her limited experience."

Adler glared at the other Councilor. "Mr. Takahashi, I really don't think—"

"Actually, I do think it's important," Haro said, cutting Adler off. "Liv's magic might normalize, or this may be something she needs to deal with before it gets out of hand."

"Wait, what?" Liv asked, looking at the two magicians. "Is everything okay?"

Haro considered for a moment and then nodded. "It's

fine, but you're presently very powerful, and we have no way of telling how long that could last."

"More powerful than I should be, or more powerful than..."

Haro nodded, sensing the words Liv hadn't said. "You're more powerful than most, and I would encourage you to continue to train in order to hone your power. You used it effectively at the museum, but it could have quickly gotten out of hand. I also think that you could benefit from other types of training. Maybe things related to combat, so that you don't always have to drain your magic. The two together could make you a formidable force."

Liv noticed Akio's eyes flicker in her direction for an instant. She bowed slightly to his brother. "I'll take that under advisement. Thank you."

At the conclusion of her words, Liv turned and left the chamber. She couldn't shake the feeling that there was something the Takahashi brothers weren't saying, and she couldn't figure out whether they could be trusted or not.

CHAPTER FIFTEEN

Liv and Plato went up to the library in complete silence. She didn't know if she'd find Sophia hiding in there again, but for some reason, she hadn't been able to shake the location out of her head since revisiting it. Every night she'd dreamed of getting lost in the aisle, and she wondered if her dreams were giving her a message.

She wasn't one to put stock in dream interpretation or dwell very long on their hidden messages. She thought that sometimes the subconsciousness needed to doodle and that was what dreams were. They didn't make any sense, and rarely were they works of art, but they released some of a person's tension. That was important.

"When are you going to tell me what you know about the white tiger and the crow?" Liv finally asked, breaking the silence.

"When do you want to know?" Plato asked coyly.

"Now would be good," Liv answered.

"If my suspicions are correct, their meaning is quite straightforward," Plato said as they reached the library.

There was no one around, but that was how it always felt in the grand space; like Liv was alone on a deserted island, safe and free to explore at her leisure.

She halted in the entrance, for a moment wanting to pay her respects as if she'd entered a chapel. It was always like she wanted to perform a ritual out of respect for the knowledge the library held. Plato glanced at her with a curious expression on his face.

Shaking off the temptation, Liv directed her attention at the cat. There must be no one around, she realized, or Plato wouldn't be out in plain sight. "So, the tiger and crow? What are your suspicions?"

"Remember what your ring has inscribed on it?" Plato asked.

"My mother's ring," she corrected. "Or Ian's ring, maybe. Not mine."

"It's in your possession now, and you are one of three remaining Beaufonts," Plato reminded her, although she wished he wouldn't have.

Liv pulled the ring from her pocket and read from it, wanting to get the phrase exactly right. "Together we are strong and balanced."

Plato nodded. "Exactly. I think the crow and the tiger are meant to keep the balance in the Chamber of the Tree."

Liv seemed to remember Clark saying something about how the tiger helped with balance, but that still didn't compute for her. "But how do they do that?"

"All things that last in life have balance," Plato began as they strolled down an aisle. They were not heading for any particular place, but rather just ambling. "Each person has a feminine and a masculine side, and we all have a

hand. She opened her fist, noting that the stones in the ring matched the indentations.

"Could this be?" Liv asked, looking over her shoulder for Plato. He wasn't there; again he'd disappeared.

"Damn cat is never there when I need him," she muttered to herself.

"Which cat do you mean?" Stefan's voice called from a nearby row of books.

Liv startled, folding her fingers over the ring and turning to face him.

Of course Plato had disappeared. He had probably known Stefan was approaching long before he reached her. *Maybe next time he'll give me a little heads up,* she thought.

"I was referring to my cat Plato, who appears to be hiding again," Liv explained, looking sideways at the groove in the wall that had caught her attention moments prior.

Stefan strode out from between two rows. He was wearing a long black jacket and traveling boots, his hair covered in a knit hat. "That's funny. I didn't know that you had a pet that is approved to enter the House of Seven."

"Rules don't really apply to Plato," she said, chewing her lip and wishing that Stefan would disappear so she could inspect the wall again.

"He sounds like he takes after you." He looked behind her, his gaze full of interest. "Did you find something on that wall? You seemed fascinated by it a moment ago."

Liv glanced casually over her shoulder. "Oh, no. I'm looking for my sister and thought she might be hiding somewhere over here. She's good with disguises."

"She'd have to be if you thought she was hiding against

a solid wall," Stefan said, sounding impressed.

Liv nearly clenched her eyes shut, thinking she'd made a grave error by giving Stefan a hint that her sister's magic had come in and was strong enough for her to do such thing as disguises. However, he continued to smile good-naturedly, the same way his sister did during meetings with the Seven. Maybe the Ludwigs could be trusted? She wasn't about to tell them everything, but having an ally might possibly prove useful.

"So where do you suppose Ms. Sophia Beaufont is hiding?" Stefan asked, looking around. "Is this a game you play, or did she run away?"

Liv laughed. "It's a game. I suspect that if Sophia wanted to run away, then she would, and none of us would ever find her. I can only discover her hiding places because she allows it."

Stefan nodded. "That seems about right. May I help you find her?"

Liv lifted a curious eyebrow at him. "Don't you have important Warrior business to attend to?"

"I do," Stefan replied, unhurried. "However, I won't set off for several more hours. Not until the timing is correct. And you? Has the Council assigned you another case to keep you busy and out of harm's way?"

"Yes, wiping fairy asses or something," Liv joked.

"And yet, you'll probably still find a way to end up on the national news while breaking a hundred laws," Stefan told her with a wink, staying beside her as they strode through the aisles. "What were you doing at the museum?"

"Brushing up on my history," Liv replied.

"And this case that was set off when you touched it? Do

you by chance want to share what was in it?"

Liv bit her lip again. She needed allies, she reminded herself again. But she didn't need troublemakers, and she wasn't sure which one Stefan Ludwig was.

After a long moment of silence, Stefan said, "It's fine, you don't have to tell me. I daresay, I have a fair number of things I like to keep secret too."

"Like what?" Liv asked at once.

He flashed a sideways smile at her. "Things."

"Thanks for revealing so much," she drawled sarcastically.

"It was curious that a case reacted to your magic like that," Stefan mused. "More curious is that certain people on the Council didn't find this of interest."

"Yeah, they seemed to simply gloss over the fact that I triggered the alarms," Liv agreed, realizing at once that Stefan was right. Then something else occurred to her. "Hey, what were the details regarding the bank vault that Adler set off? Do you know?"

Stefan shook his head. "That was the first I'd heard of it, but it is interesting. We have our own banking systems within the House as you very well know, so I wonder what he was doing at a mortal-owned bank."

"Another thing that the Council sort of glossed over," Liv said mostly to herself.

"Questions that Adler doesn't want asked have a way of being ignored," Stefan offered.

They paused in the center of a large reading area. Huge overstuffed chairs sat around a fireplace that was taller than Stefan. Liv blinked at the painting above the fireplace, recognizing the little girl standing next to a tall palomino.

She nearly paused, surprised by the sight of her little sister disguised in an oil painting, but she stopped herself, pointing to an aisle.

"Let's see if Sophia is down here," she said in a rush. "If not, hopefully she comes out of her hiding place soon." She said the last part with a heavy inflection in her voice, intending that her sister get the hint.

"Weren't you and Trudy hunting unregistered magicians together?" Liv asked when they'd walked in silence for a moment.

"Yes," Stefan answered. "However, I got assigned a different case, and I think she got a little sloppy, hence the excitement today."

Liv nearly shivered with disgust. "Hunting down our own and punishing them for not registering their magic seems so wrong. I can't imagine having to do it."

Stefan agreed with a nod. "I'm glad to have a different case, although I wish I had been there to help Trudy. Maybe I could have kept her out of trouble."

"Because you would have done all the slaying of innocent magicians for her?" Liv teased, defiance written on her face.

A roguish smile crossed Stefan's lips. "Yeah, something like that."

Secrets. Stefan Ludwig definitely had his fair share of secrets, and Liv desperately wanted to know what some of them were. Maybe it was the serious look in his bright blue eyes or the mysteries that seemed to dance behind the surface of his expression. She decided to play a game of reciprocation and see if that worked to open things up.

"So the case I touched at the museum," Liv began.

"The one with the mystery contents that you can't disclose?" Stefan asked.

She waved him off. "It's not really important. But do you know why a case in a mortals' museum would be protected by magic?"

"You said that you set off an alarm," Stefan said. "You never mentioned that it had magical wards."

"That part must have slipped my mind during the meeting with the Seven," Liv explained, tilting her head and trying to look like a ditz.

"That sort of thing happens to me all the time during those meetings," Stefan said, and then looked down. "But remember that your magic is monitored through the Council, so be careful. They might not be able to see what you're doing all the time, but they can piece things together. That's why understanding how to use your magic in general ways is important."

Liv nodded, looking into the distance without seeing as all this sunk in. If she used her magic to perform any opening spells, the Council would see that, as they had at the museum. However, if she employed a more general spell, they wouldn't have a clue what she was doing.

"It doesn't make any sense why there would be magic protecting anything in the Natural History Museum," Stefan said, tapping his fingers on his lips as he thought. "I've never heard of such a thing. How did you discover this?"

"I'm good at finding these things out, apparently," Liv stated. "I search out trouble."

Stefan laughed. "That you do. And it looks like you also find adorable magicians." He pointed to a large couch that sat against a muraled wall. In the center of the couch and covered in overstuffed pillows was a bulky form. Protruding from under the pillows were two little feet in white tights and black, patent leather shoes.

Liv nearly burst out laughing at the horrible hiding spot. Sophia was too much, even while pretending to be a simple child playing a regular game of hide-and-seek.

"Oh, right. I wonder where Sophia is," Liv said loudly, which prompted a giggle from the pillows.

Liv flashed Stefan a smile. "I guess she's not here."

More giggles made the pillows dance.

"That's too bad, because if she were, I'd have a present for her," Stefan announced.

Sophia burst from the couch, landing on her feet with her arms wide, the pillows tumbling to the ground. Just like in the painting, she wore a blue velvet dress and her soft, curly hair was pulled back into a low ponytail.

"Soph!" Liv exclaimed. "You were right there. I had no idea."

"Present," Sophia demanded. "I was promised a present. I heard it."

Stefan laughed and went down on one knee. "And I'm a man of my word. It's important that you always remember that. If I tell you something, you can rest assured that it's true." His eyes flicked up to meet Liv's briefly before he opened his hand to reveal a soft blue rose petal.

"Is that…" Sophia asked, her wide eyes looking between Stefan and the object in his hand.

He nodded. "It is. A rare but authentic depour."

"Wow! I've never seen one in person." Sophia's hand paused as she went to grab for it. "Is it really mine?"

Stefan nodded, carefully dropping it into her palm. "Yes, but be gentle with it, and remember it can only be used once."

The little girl beamed, her bright eyes lighting up. "I can't believe it! I'm going to go turn our living area into a winter wonderland! Oh, Clark will be so angry."

Before Liv could ask Sophia a question, she was off, streaking through the library with her long ponytail flying behind her.

"Ummm, what's a depour?" Liv asked Stefan.

"Remember when I said it's good to do general magic if you don't want to be tracked?" he asked. "Well, there are also magical objects you can obtain that will do things for you that can't be traced back to you. A depour is one of them. I just gave your sister one that will create a great deal of snow in an area. Sounds like she's going to turn the Beaufont residence into a ski lodge for the evening."

Liv laughed. "Oh, Clark will be so pissed. And how do I get hold of one of these depours?"

Stefan considered her for a moment. "There are different kinds. Red ones create fire. Blue ones, snow, and purple, rain. You get the idea. And you have to know the right people."

"And by people you mean..."

"Elves," Stefan answered. "The elves are the ones who create the depours. But you'll learn all this in time. And I'm always happy to help, like with this museum project you're working on."

Liv considered him for a moment and shook her head. "Thank you, but no. I think I'm better operating alone on this one."

CHAPTER SIXTEEN

"I don't know when you found the time," John said, his hands on his hips as he gazed fondly around the shop. It was clean. No, it was more than clean. If Liv didn't know any better, she'd think it was brand new.

"I didn't find the time," Liv admitted.

The smile on John's face vanished. "This wasn't you? You weren't the one who cleaned the shop last night?"

Liv wanted to avoid the speculation and say it was her, but she couldn't take credit for what the brownies had done. In truth, they had done a better job in John's shop than they normally would have. Usually, a brownie merely did a few chores, making the mortal's schedule a little easier. Mortimer must have been extremely happy with their agreement and was trying to show it.

"If this wasn't you, then who?" John asked, concern suddenly appearing on his face.

"Maybe those same thugs who broke in before did it again, but this time decided to make up for their misdeeds?" Liv suggested.

John rolled his eyes. "No, I'm not buying that some hoodlums came in here and polished the floor and relabeled the shelves last night."

Yeah, this brownie went entirely too far. He was going to make it impossible for Liv to not tell John the truth.

"Maybe it was Rory," Liv supplied. "You know how he likes to do things for you."

John nodded. "Yeah, maybe, but I don't know when, since he was working at the Sunshine Nursing Home last night."

"He was *what?*" Liv asked.

John's lips pressed together. "Well, you shouldn't say anything. He looked a little mortified when I found him there. I'd gone over to drop off a coffee pot that I had repaired for Mr. Jeremiah Grimes. I didn't think that Rory would have to pick up extra work. Thought he was doing all right, but it just goes to show that the cost of living here in LA has everyone working doubly hard."

Liv narrowed her eyes, considering this. "Working, you say? Are you sure he wasn't volunteering?"

John scratched his mostly bald head. "Now, why would he do that? Nah, I'm sure he was working. And you should have seen him with the old folks." A chuckle fell from John's mouth. "As gentle as a—"

"Don't you even dare," Liv said, cutting him off.

"Well, you get the idea. And I know he isn't a giant. It's just genes, and whatever his mother ate when she was pregnant with him."

"Kittens," Liv stated.

"Say what?" John asked, leaning forward like he hadn't heard her properly.

"His mother ate kittens."

This made Pickles break into a sudden flurry of barking as if he had taken offense to the joke.

John waved her off. "Oh, you're too silly."

His eyes suddenly turned serious. "Why didn't you ever tell me you had a brother?"

Liv deflated. She should have seen this conversation coming. Plato cracked an eye open and peered at her for a moment before shutting it again.

"You remember when we first met?" Liv asked John.

He nodded and froze. "Yeah, you'd just lost…"

"My parents had died," she said, picking up where he'd left off. "It was a dark time for me."

"I figured you were all alone." John picked up Pickles and petted him fondly before looking at Liv again. "You never mentioned a brother, and I just assumed you didn't have any other family."

John had never pried, and Liv had respected that about him. It was one of the many reasons it was easy to keep working at the repair shop. Back then, she hadn't thought she could answer questions.

"I also have a little sister," Liv offered.

"You don't say?" John's face brightened. "I learn something new every day. Will I get the pleasure of meeting her?"

Liv shook her head. "Not anytime soon. She's in a boarding school of sorts."

"Of sorts?" John questioned.

"Well, just a boarding school, but it's one of those weird ones where they have rigid curriculums and the teachers use fancy words, and she can't really leave except on holidays," Liv explained.

A sour expression crossed John's face. "Oh, I know the type. How is a child supposed to breathe and be creative in a place like that?"

Liv smiled inwardly. "Sophia manages."

"I do believe I've learned more about you in the last week than I have in a long time," John stated.

"Yeah, well, I'm trying. I can't always be a closed book."

"You be what you want to be, and the rest of us will accept that," John said, suddenly stern. "It isn't good for you to live your life on everyone else's terms. And hell, no one can be happy living like that."

And there it was. This was exactly why Liv adored the man.

John set Pickles down and strode over to the cash register, looking it over like he had lost something. "Whatever happened to this place, I can't find a darn thing." He chuckled, opening the register and pushing notes around, craning to look in the back of the drawer.

"What are you looking for?" Liv asked.

"I just remembered that some fella came by looking for you last night," John said, continuing to shuffle things around. "Real good-looking guy, but I forget what his name was."

"What? Are you sure he was looking for me?"

John laughed. "Yeah, there is only one Liv Beaufont here. I guess he'd tried you at your other job, but he said he didn't know exactly where that was. He asked me about it, but I told him it was none of my business, nor his."

John's face brightened as he pulled a piece of paper out of the register. "Here it is! I promise I didn't read it."

Liv reached over and grabbed the note a bit more urgently than she meant to. She nearly tore it in two opening it. There was only one line:

Your agreement to have a drink with me is binding. – Rudolf

Liv reread it five times, swearing that her ability to read had failed her and she was misunderstanding the message. Plato had gotten up from his nap and perched on the table close enough that he could read the message. She'd love to know what he thought it meant, but she didn't dare glance at him with John staring at her.

"Ummm… This guy, Rudolf—he came into the shop yesterday?" Liv asked, trying to act casual.

"Oh, yes," John stated. "Does he work with your brother in the acting troupe? He was wearing the most peculiar costume—this red getup. I think it was crushed velvet. Haven't seen anything like that since the eighties. I hope it's not making a comeback."

"Sure, yeah, Rudolf is an actor too," Liv said, grateful to have John supply an excuse. "Besides the costume, did he look weird?"

John thought for a moment. "Well, he was the most handsome man I've seen in a while, but if you tell anyone I said that, I'll deny it flatly."

So he'd glamoured his wings and ears. Good, Liv thought.

"Rudolf isn't all that handsome once you have a conversation with him," Liv said.

"Well, still, if you need to go see him or your brother or do whatever, I can watch the shop for the rest of the day." John looked around. "Actually, thanks to that magical force that cleaned the place up last night, I don't have a thing to do."

Liv's eyes widened at the mention of magic. She was about to say something when she noticed the words scrolling across the back of the register. Usually, after a transaction, they read, Thank You for Your Business. Have a Great Day.

However, presently they read, Liv Beaufont's presence is requested on Roya Lane. Canister Seen.

"You know what, I think I will take you up on your offer," Liv said in a rush, grabbing her bag and slinging it across her back. She was out the door before John could say another word.

CHAPTER SEVENTEEN

"What does he mean by binding agreement?" Liv asked as she hurried in and threw her bag down in her still-messy apartment. She could really have used some help from a brownie, but she guessed if she took an extra minute, she could clean the whole place using magic.

Plato poked his head out of her bag, which he'd stowed away in just prior to her leaving John's shop. "Did you make an agreement with the fae?"

Liv thought for a moment. "I don't think so. He just insulted me several times, and I made idle threats."

"It could be as simple as a question," Plato explained. "Fae take their agreements very seriously, and will hold you to them."

"Or what?" Liv asked, her heart pounding in her chest. She needed to go see Mortimer, but it would be helpful if she knew what mess she'd gotten herself into with Rudolf.

"Or you have to pay their price, which is usually high and considered extremely unfair." Plato licked his paw, not appearing at all ruffled by Liv's plight.

"But I don't remember agreeing to anything," she explained, her voice turning shrill.

"That's the thing," Plato said. "If you would have asked me, I would have warned you to stay away from the fae. They are incredibly deceptive creatures. One minute you're having a casual conversation, and the next you've promised them your first-born without realizing it."

"Well, where were *you* when Rudolf offered his help and conned me into a conversation with him?"

"I was nearby, and I remember the whole thing rather clearly."

"Then tell me what I agreed to," Liv urged.

Plato ran his wet paw over his head. "I don't recall that part, to be honest. Just shows that it must have been expertly worded."

Liv sighed. "Great. Now I'm in a binding agreement with a fae, and John is growing more suspicious about what's going on around the shop. How am I supposed to keep him in the dark with fae showing up at my work and my magician brother stopping by the shop? Oh, and Rory pretending he's just a very large man?"

Plato nodded. "I fear it's only going to get worse for you. Hiding the magic in your life won't be easy, not now that you're a Warrior."

"Well, I'm not quitting my job," Liv said flatly.

"Then you might want to consider compartmentalizing your life a bit."

Liv eyed the cat for a moment. "Yeah, maybe. But not right now." She created a portal to Roya Lane and stepped through.

"Oh good, you got my note," Rudolf said as soon as Liv set foot on the cobbled street. He looked her up and down, a dissatisfied expression on his face. "Really, you could have worn something a bit more provocative."

Liv peered down at her black leather pants and jacket. "What's wrong with this?"

"It's so overrated. All the wannabe heroines wear that outfit."

"Well, there you go," Liv stated matter-of-factly. "I'm not a wannabe heroine, I'm a reluctant Warrior."

"Still, it's an awful choice for where I'm taking you," Rudolf said, holding his finger in the air and tracing her form. "Let me put you in a ball gown. Maybe something from the sixteenth century with a corset that controls your—"

"Finish that sentence and I'll put your head through a sieve," Liv threatened.

Rudolf held up his hands in surrender. "Okay, so no corset. I don't really think you need it."

Liv blinked at the fae dully for a moment and then scanned the area around him. Roya Lane was just as packed as before, and there were still strange interactions happening between various races of magical creatures. "What is this binding agreement I entered into with you?"

Rudolf laughed. "Oh, a magician's memory is a fickle little thing. I forget that you don't have the benefit of the fae's powers of recollection. We live so long that our memories become rather exceptional, helping us to keep up with all the things mortals and magical creatures promise us."

Liv stuck her fists on her hips. "I didn't promise you anything."

Rudolf held up a finger and wagged it. "Oh, but you did, Ms. Liv Beaufont, Warrior of the House of Seven. Before you entered the brownies official headquarters, I said, 'We should grab a drink sometime,' to which you agreed."

Liv narrowed her eyes at the man before her. "*That's* what this is about? A stupid drink? I have real responsibilities and things to deal with, and no time to sit across a table from you and listen to your insults."

Rudolf laughed as if she'd told a charming joke. "Oh, I agree that time for you is dwindling. What do you have—a hundred, maybe two hundred years? That was why I went to see you at the shop where you work; to ensure you didn't forget and pay the price of ignoring our agreement."

"First of all, don't go back to that shop unless you want me to spend the rest of my remaining years on this Earth trying to figure out how to end your life," Liv stated. "And secondly, what dumb price would I pay if I didn't go and have a drink with you?"

Rudolf glanced at his fingernails like they suddenly were of great interest to him. "Let's see, a disregarded level-three agreement would cost you a dozen years of servitude to me."

Liv laughed, making a group of sour-looking gnomes turn around to scowl at her. "I'm already serving a dozen-year sentence at the House of Seven, so go ahead and get in line."

Rudolf dropped his hand and smiled discreetly at her.

"I'm afraid fae law trumps that of magicians. The last magician who tried to get out of one of our agreements and appealed to the House found himself abandoned, and he is still paying our high prices. There is simply nothing the House can do to us, although they try every century."

"This is very fascinating and all, but I actually have business with the brownies," Liv stated. "I'll have to take a raincheck for that drink. Say in about a hundred years?"

Rudolf puffed out his pink lips and clicked his tongue three times. "I'm afraid that won't work. You have until the end of today to make good on our agreement or I'll have to enforce the fine print."

A growl escaped Liv's mouth. "How can there be any fine print when I didn't sign anything?"

The fae gave her a sinister glare. "That's the beauty of our agreements. They are full of all sorts of fine print that you never read but is set in stone. You agreed to have a drink with me, and are obligated to do so. Otherwise, I'll be sad to see you become my chambermaid, but grateful that I'll have the company of your face for the next dozen years."

Liv couldn't believe that she was about to jeopardize her family's place in the House of Seven once again. She couldn't lose her position because of something silly with this Fae. If she became a slave to this self-absorbed dimwit, the Beaufonts would be removed from the Seven, and it would be all her fault.

"Fine. Can I meet you in an hour or so somewhere?" Liv said, defeat heavy in her voice. "I've presently got a meeting I have to attend."

"I could go with you," Rudolf offered, his face tilted to the side.

Liv shook her head quickly. "Nope. But I'll meet you wherever you want." Catching the mischievous look on Rudolf's face, Liv shook her head more forcefully. "Any pub on Roya Lane that you want. No weird brothel-type places or whatever other gross establishments you have in mind."

Rudolf's grin fell away. "Oh, too bad. I know of some devilishly good places. Alas, I'll meet you at the Wishing Well."

"That better be a legit bar and not some fae trickery," Liv warned.

Rudolf nodded. "It's completely innocent—a simple pub run by elves. Quite boring, but I'll be there. That always makes it interesting."

"Fine, but one drink and then I'm done with you, right?" Liv asked.

"For now," Rudolf said with a wink.

Before all this magic business, Liv would have had time to watch Netflix and veg on nachos. Her stomach rumbled furiously as she made her way down the hallway to Mortimer's office. She hadn't eaten enough today, and it was starting to take a toll on her. Maybe if she crammed chips piled high with meat and cheese ungracefully into her mouth, Rudolf would leave her alone for the rest of her seemingly short life.

Liv knocked and simultaneously opened the door to the

brownie's office. He wasn't behind his desk when she entered, as she'd expected.

"Umm...hello?"

"I'm here," a squeaky voice called from behind a stack of books and papers in the corner.

"Are you okay?" Liv asked, trying to peer around the mess to find the brownie.

"I'm fine," Mortimer answered. "Just sorting. Applebee, go over here. Smuthers, here. And Carnago, here." Papers slipped onto the tops of three different stacks that were nearly touching the ceiling.

"Ha-ha-ha*chu!*" The brownie's sneeze sent the stacks in all directions, papers spiraling through the air. Liv shielded her face, accosted by a barrage of paper that struck her lightly.

"Oh, pond scum!" Mortimer exclaimed, looking around as the papers settled on the floor. "That's the third time that's happened."

"You're joking, right?" Liv asked.

He stared at her seriously. "What do you mean? Of course, I'm not. I've caught an awful cold, and it keeps messing up my attempts at filing."

"Might you consider a different system?" Liv offered. "Maybe one where you don't file the papers on precarious stacks that tower up to the ceiling?"

The brownie blinked at her as if she were a sudden apparition, then laughed. "You're a funny magician. Thanks, I needed the laugh."

Liv shook off this strange behavior and knelt to help Mortimer pick up the papers. Strangely, there was nothing written on them. They were all blank, but he kept muttering to himself as if they weren't.

"Forkspeed goes over here, and Sleuthgrove over here," he said, retrieving the papers and reassembling the stacks.

"You sent a message for me to see you," Liv stated. "Have you found something?"

Mortimer looked up from his filing, his wrinkled face full of confusion. Apparently he'd momentarily forgotten that she was there. "Oh, right. Yes, but nothing much yet. One of my brownies said they'd seen a canister of magic enter a dwelling they clean."

Liv's fingers nearly crumpled the paper she was holding. "What? That's great news. Where is it?"

"Uttercert goes here, and Loylolla over here."

"Mortimer!"

The brownie looked up suddenly. "Right, right. You're still here. I always get lost in the task when filing."

"Well, maybe you can pause for just a moment. This is important. The canister?"

"Yes, good news. It's been spotted. The bad news is that the brownie I spoke with can't remember where."

Liv deflated. "Really? How is that possible?"

"I assure you that it's very possible. We brownies clean many a home in a night sometimes. Hundreds of homes a year, and over a—"

"I get it," Liv said, cutting him off.

Mortimer's large eyes fell on the paper in his hands and he began to read.

"So what do we do?" Liv asked, trying to keep him focused.

"I've got him thinking about it," Mortimer replied,

undeterred. "I suspect the location will occur to him some-time soon. But I wanted to give you the good news."

Liv stuck the papers she'd gathered on the overflowing desk, careful to stay hunched so she didn't hit her head. "I'm not sure that is good news."

"Well, that's not all of it," Mortimer said. It appeared to be quite difficult for him to keep himself from continuing to file; his gaze drifted back down to the papers in his hands.

Liv picked up the green ball on his desk and tossed it in the air. That grabbed his attention, making him drop the stack of papers and waddle over to where she was. He held out his palm flatly, a demanding look on his face.

She set the foam ball in his hand and smiled down at him. "Please tell me more, then."

"Well, I got to thinking about your predicament with the giant's sword protected by magic," Mortimer began, striding around his desk, slipping on papers and nearly falling. "Your little incident in the Natural History Museum didn't go unnoticed by my brownies."

"Or a few others, it would seem," Liv stated dully.

"Anyway, once we knew the location you were refer-ring to, I had my brownies do some investigating," Mortimer said. He started to throw the ball at the door and catch it again. "One. Two. Three."

"What did they learn?" Liv asked, nearly flinching every time the ball whizzed dangerously close to her face.

"That the lower lobby is a complete pig's pen," Mortimer said, throwing the ball faster as if he was suddenly charged by the topic. "There's a fine layer of dust on the animal exhibit, and there's a case of tools that is absolutely disgusting."

"I meant, what did they find out about the sword?" Liv asked. "Or were they overwhelmed by the unkempt exhibits?"

"Nearly. Museums aren't generally under the brownies' jurisdiction. Mostly it's homes. Sometimes stores, as in the case of your friend John's shop. But museums don't belong to a person per se, so they don't get our attention. There are rare examples of groups of residents in nursing homes and similar places, but not usually public places such as that one."

"Although this is fascinating," Liv began, "I'm wondering if your brownie found anything of use, or is this another case where they know something but can't remember it?"

Mortimer paused before throwing the ball again. "I think you'll be pleased to know that they learned that although the wards prevent giants from trespassing into the sword room, and prevented you from touching the case, that same magic doesn't work on brownies."

Liv didn't breathe for several seconds. Only once Mortimer continued throwing the ball did she cough out a breath. "So the brownies can get to the sword? Does that mean that they will?"

Mortimer paused and looked at her seriously. "Are you asking us to aid you in an effort to steal a sword that belongs to mortals?"

"Well, no, but… I mean, you said yourself that you have no loyalty to the particular mortals who run the museum. And the sword does belong—"

Mortimer held up his hand to stop her. "The less I know, the better. All I know is that Liv Beaufont treats brownies with consideration, not pressing her rule upon us like so many Warriors before her. Also, we watch you at John's shop, and you have a true heart. Although you're not a mortal, we think of you fondly."

"Thank you?" Liv responded tentatively.

"So, yes," Mortimer said with an expression that sort of resembled a smile. "I agree that my brownies will help you get the sword from the museum, but you should know that even with their help, it's going to be a very risky venture."

Liv nodded, having sensed that was going to be the case. And if she was caught a second time breaking into that museum *and* with the help of brownies, Adler was going to have her head—or her magic.

"If we can secure the sword, I'll take the risk," Liv stated confidently.

Mortimer picked up a single piece of paper from the chaos on his desk and handed it to her. "Then you should see this. I've drafted a plan that I think will work if you can pull off the rest."

Liv's eyes scanned the paper briefly, and her mouth fell open. "Damn. It will be a miracle if we pull this off."

Mortimer agreed as he continued to throw the ball. "This sword must mean a great deal to you to go to such great lengths. Does that mean you agree to the plan?"

Liv glanced at the paper one more time. "Yeah, let's do it!"

CHAPTER EIGHTEEN

L iv halted inside the Wishing Well. She shouldn't have been surprised to find a well in the middle of the pub, with fairies filling little cups up from it and flying them off to patrons, and yet she couldn't look away. The ceiling had been enchanted to look like a starry sky, and the walls were painted in rolling meadows that went on for miles. The music that rose from the piano in the corner was a bit too whimsical for her liking, but she still found herself swaying to the beat.

"Does my lady approve of this place?" Rudolf asked, appearing suddenly beside Liv.

A tiny fairy holding a harp began to twirl around Liv's head as she played, her giggling accompanying the music.

Liv swatted at her like she was a fly. "Yeah, no. Can we go someplace that doesn't make me want to throw up?"

"But they have chocolate-dipped..." Rudolf, reading the expression on her face, let his voice trail off. "Yeah, that's fine. Maybe something in your neck of the woods?"

Liv rolled her eyes. "The pun is not appreciated," she

said, eyeing the seemingly real trees that towered around the pub. "There's a bar down the street from my house. It's called No More Heroes."

Rudolf's face contorted with distaste. "What kind of place is that? I'm not sure I approve."

"Well, those are the terms of *my* agreement," Liv said simply, creating a portal and looking back at him before stepping through. "Either you join me or the deal is off."

"I don't understand the décor," Rudolf said when they entered the bar. It was non-pretentious. Minimalistic. Warm and inviting.

Long tables with small stools ran the length of the space, and the green booths that lined the wall looked as old as the paisley wallpaper.

"Where is the flowing river of apple cider or the centaur that spits wine into your mouth?" Rudolf asked, striding behind Liv as she found them a place at the bar. Most of the women turned to eye him, giving the fae appreciative looks.

"It's not that kind of place," Liv stated, hopping up on the stool. "What you see is what you get here." She sighed, enjoying being in a normal place with normal people.

The guy next to her turned around and gave her an apologetic look. "Oh, you can't sit there. My aura needs a bit of extra space today. It's feeling fat."

Well, *sort* of normal. LA normal, as if that were a thing. Liv shook her head at the hipster. "Tell it too bad. This is my seat."

He bristled but turned back to his date without argument.

"I'm happy to fight for your honor, my lady," Rudolf

said, pulling out a seat and looking between her and the hipster.

She shook her head. "No one fights with hipsters. If you do, you run the risk of wrinkling their shirt or scuffing their Doc Martens, and the whining never stops after that. It's better to ignore them. They're afraid of their own shadows and anything from last year."

"This mortal lifestyle you live is very strange," Rudolf said, sliding onto the barstool.

Liv held up her hand to the bartender, a slender lady who had hair extensions and was wearing a tight shirt that read Certified Organic.

She ignored Liv, sending drinks over to a couple who were chatting animatedly as they watched something on one of their phones.

"So, why exactly did you make me go out with you?" Liv asked, looking at the fae.

His eyes bounced around the various patrons in the bar before looking directly at her. "Most would find this to be a great honor, and yet you see it as an obligation."

Liv's stomach rumbled, and she tried again to get the bimbo-bartender's attention.

"I remember that when I was your age, I took for granted the attention of elders such as I," Rudolf continued.

"Wait, now I'm young?" Liv asked. "I thought I was on the brink of being too old and withered for you?"

"Oh, that day will come, my love. That day will come, and unfortunately, not long from now. But we have tonight." Rudolf reached out and tried to run his fingers through Liv's hair but she blocked, him, knocking his arm to the bar. She pinned it down, making it impossible for him to move.

"If you ever touch me again, I will pluck each of your long eyelashes out with my teeth and feed them to seagulls. Are we clear?"

Rudolf retracted his arm, a scorned look on his face. "My lady, I think you misunderstand my gestures. I only mean to make you swoon and fall irrevocably in love with me."

Liv turned to face the bar. "Yeah, I don't think I will." She tried again to get the bartender's attention, with no luck. "Damn it! Am I invisible?"

"If you are, it's the worst invisibility spell I've ever seen," Rudolf said, waving his fingers slightly. The bartender looked up as if someone had shouted her name, her attention landing directly on the fae. She set down the drinks she was in the middle of making and hurried over.

"Hello, my dear mortal," Rudolf began, his tone melodic.

"What can I get for you?" the woman asked, bending low over the bar, her cleavage popping out.

Rudolf leaned away and waved in Liv's direction. "Whatever my saucy friend would like."

Liv slapped her hand on the bar. "About damn time. Yes, I'd like nachos, and not spa nachos with cauliflower and vegan cheese. I want the real thing. And a side of fries. A rum and coke. No, make it two rum and cokes. Oh, and a side of bacon. No, make it two sides of bacon."

Not having written down anything, the bartender looked at Rudolf. "For you, sir?"

"I'll have water," he said politely. "You do have that here? Is it safe to drink?"

She giggled as if he'd told a joke. "Of course. This isn't North Hollywood."

Liv refused to talk to the fae until she'd crammed three strips of bacon into her mouth and finished her first rum and coke. Feeling more herself, she glanced at Rudolf, who was regarding her with a serene smile.

"You are the freshest specimen I've set my eyes on in a very long time!" he told her, leaning his head on his palm and gazing longingly at her.

Liv wiped her mouth with the back of her sleeve and burped loudly, making several nearby patrons turn and give her rude stares.

"What exactly is your deal?" she asked, pushing the empty plate of bacon out of the way to make way for the pile of nachos that was the size of a small bulldog.

"Actually, that's the reason I asked you on this date."

"It's not a date," she responded, picking the best place to attack the nachos from. "And you didn't ask. You demanded, and then sent a threatening note to my place of work."

Rudolf watched as Liv crammed three chips into her mouth at once. "What business do you have with the brownies?"

"Reg-tion tip tuf," she said with her mouth still full.

He nodded. "Oh, right. You're going to have me believe that you're working on House business, are you?"

"Why else would I squeeze my ass through those tiny doors and sit in a dusty office with a smelly elf?"

"It has occurred to me, Ms. Liv Beaufont, Warrior of the

House of Seven, that you are different from most magicians," Rudolf said, picking up his water glass and eyeing it. Then, seemingly thinking better of it, he set it back down. "What is your story, and how may I help you?"

Liv shook her head, pushing the nachos away, feeling her stomach expand. "Oh, no. I know better now than to enter into any agreement with you."

"Not all agreements with a fae are bad," he reasoned. "Is it so terrible that you're in my presence now?"

"Well, I just lost my appetite, so yes."

"That's because you've had enough bacon to kill a horse," Rudolf informed her.

"Horses don't eat bacon," Liv stated.

"My point is that since I've seen that ring of yours, well, it's caused a certain reaction in me."

Liv straightened. "Wait, *that's* your point? That wasn't what you were saying a second ago. I didn't know any of this was about my ring."

"Well, you do now," Rudolf said definitively. "And it's true. I can't recall the memory linked to that ring, and that bothers me very much. I almost feel as though, well, I have an excellent memory, but it feels as though I've forgotten something. And it's not a regrettable decision like making out with an elf or playing hopscotch with a gnome. Oh, no, this feels like something I forgot without meaning to."

Liv leaned forward and grabbed Rudolf's shirt, pulling him closer. "Are you serious? Like there's something someone covered up?"

Rudolf didn't seem to mind her forceful gesture. He actually leaned closer to her. "I do like your style, but wish we were in a more fitting setting. Preferably my place? Yours, I suspect, is much too small for such activities."

Liv pushed him away. "Be serious. What are you trying to tell me?"

Rudolf straightened his tunic. "I'm not entirely sure. I was uncertain whether to say anything at all. However, you seem to be an honorable magician, and I did respect your family once. And I suppose this is a mystery we all need to solve since my suspicion is that it involves us all, or at least more than just you and the magicians."

Liv turned and faced him directly. "So, are you saying you're going to help me?"

He thought for a moment. "I'm not sure what I'm helping you with."

"The ring," Liv stated, pulling it from her pants and showing it to him. "I know it's supposed to tell me something. Maybe multiple somethings. And if it causes a reaction in you, then there might be all sorts of things it will uncover. But I'm new to this, and I don't know where to look. And now you're saying it made you remember something you forgot. I think that's worth investigating."

Rudolf's gaze stayed on the ring for a long moment, then he looked at her directly. "I think you're right, Liv. I think that there is much the ring can tell you."

"Will you help me?"

His eyebrow arched as he gave her a wolfish grin. "Be careful what you ask from a fae."

Liv sank back on her stool. "Never mind, then. I can't afford to be your servant for a dozen years or whatever you'd have me do."

She was putting the ring back in her pocket when

Rudolf reached out and grabbed her hand. "This isn't an agreement. You have my word on that. I suspect there is something at play much bigger than you, or maybe even me. For that reason, yes, Liv Beaufont, Warrior of the House of Seven, I will try to help you."

Liv stared at the fae for several long seconds before nodding. "So what does that mean?"

He released her hand. "I'm not certain yet. I'll try to remember what I have forgotten—the memory associated with the ring. I'll do what I can, but I fear I might remember a hundred years too late, and that will do you no good since you'll be—"

"Old and gray," Liv said, cutting him off. "Yeah, that's a chance I'll have to take." She held out her hand to him. "And you have yourself a deal."

He didn't take her hand but rather smiled widely at her. "Oh, a deal means we mutually benefit. So what is it that you offer, my sweet?"

"What is it that you want?" Liv asked. "And if you say my servitude or firstborn, no deal."

"Something that has long resided in the House of Seven," Rudolf answered. "Upon the time that I remember that which I've been forced to forget—a memory I believe has been erased from the minds of all fae and other creatures alike—I ask that you reunite me with the treasure that lives in the ponds of the House of Seven."

Liv waited for Rudolf to laugh and say he was just kidding. When he didn't, she lowered her chin and said, "Are you flipping serious? You want me to reunite you with that monster? It once tried to drown me."

"I wouldn't call it a monster," Rudolf countered. "It's a

small trinket, taken away from me long ago. I know it resides at the bottom of the pond, although the wards on the House of Seven prevent me from getting to it myself. But you... You could dive down there and get it for me."

"And face the monster," Liv reminded him.

He nodded. "Yes. It will be difficult for you, but it's a fair deal. My memories will shine a light on what you need to know, and freeing that creature will be good for all."

Liv didn't know what possessed her, but she extended her hand and offered it to Rudolf. "Fine. You have yourself a deal."

"His servant," Liv said, cutting *him* off this time.

"You're not taking this seriously enough," Rory said, more worked up than she'd ever seen him. "The fae aren't to be messed with. The fact that you spoke to him in the first place is worrisome. You should have known better."

"In my defense, he spoke to me first," Liv said, watching as two kittens wrestled on the hearth of the fireplace. Finally she pulled her gaze away and held up the ring again. "What do you think about the wall with the grooves in the library?"

Rory relinquished a bit of his anger and sighed. "I'm not sure. You're going to have to check it out more thoroughly, but make sure you're not watched. That's important."

Liv nodded. "Yeah, I agree. I'll try to stop by there tonight before the heist and check it out."

Rory's head flipped up suddenly. "Heist?"

"Yeah, I partnered with brownies to break into the Natural History Museum. No big deal. Just risking my life for something you hold valuable."

"Well, don't get caught," Rory stated matter-of-factly. "I want that sword."

"Your consideration and concern are overwhelming," Liv joked.

"You're a big girl and can handle yourself."

"Funny that you berate me for making a deal with a fae but don't even blink when you learn that I'm working with other magical creatures on a major break-in."

"Fae can't be trusted," Rory stated. "Brownies don't have any side agendas. They are simply dumb creatures. And your mission to recover the sword is important—"

"It's important to you," Liv cut in.

"And need I remind you that you made a deal with a fae for something that's intangible? A memory? You might be reading more into this ring and the conspiracies you think the House is hiding than is really there."

"You don't think the House is hiding something?" Liv asked.

"I think they are protecting their own asses with outdated laws that serve only them," Rory stated. "That's all I know."

"Well, I can't argue with you there."

"However, the sword is a tangible object, and once you retrieve it, you'll be given something in return. That's a fair deal. I won't punish you if you don't make good on your end. That's how fair deals work, but fae don't have the same moral structure as the rest of us."

"Do giants like *any* other magical creatures?" Liv asked. "Magicians are corrupt. Brownies are dumb. Fae are untrustworthy. Lynxes are deceptive."

Rory took a seat in his armchair, which was covered with handwoven blankets. "The truth is that all species have their shortcomings. If you can recognize what those are, then you can be on guard. That's not being cynical. It's being conscientious and careful."

"What are the giants' shortcomings?"

"Too much patience for magicians."

"Ha-ha," Liv said with no real humor in her voice. "Hey, I meant to ask, what are you doing working at that nursing home?"

Rory froze. His eyes were careful as he considered his reply. "You heard about that?"

"Yes, and after reflecting on the information, I've concluded that you're volunteering there out of the kindness of your heart."

"I'm not volunteering," he argued.

"But when I asked John about it, he said you were wearing a visitor's badge, which would mean—"

"I'm collecting the tears of the elderly," Rory interrupted. "It's a key ingredient for a powerful potion."

Liv narrowed her eyes at him. "Nope. You already told me that giants don't mess with potions."

"Well, I've decided to start," he said dryly, glaring at her impatiently. "There's a small pest in my life that I'm trying to exterminate."

Liv wagged her finger at him. "I haven't figured out your game yet, but I'm going to."

"I think your energy can be better spent."

Grabbing her bag off the couch, Liv fastened it on her back. "Yeah, probably, but I like the idea of figuring out your secrets. For now, I'm going to go prepare for tonight's mission to recover your grandfather's sword."

Rory held up his hand to stop her. "Although I appreciate your motivation on this project, please note that actually recovering the sword will take a long time. I've spent years trying to break those wards, and my expectation is that it will take you even longer to get past them."

Liv scoffed at the giant. "Well, you should go get to work on the sword you're making as my reward because I plan on taking back Turbinger tonight."

Rory moved only a step, but it was enough to block Liv's path to the door. "Be careful, Liv. You don't have to rush this. I've gone my entire life without that sword. Another few years are nothing."

Liv looked up at the giant, pure conviction in her eyes. "Sounds like you're overdue to have it in your possession. And don't worry about me. I've got tiny elves watching my back."

CHAPTER TWENTY

I t took Liv a lot longer than she would have liked to find the wall with the symbols in the library in the House of Seven. Even more frustrating was that the area wasn't vacant, as she would have desired.

"Are you looking for Sophia again?" Stefan asked, sitting in a high-back chair, his boots propped on an ottoman.

Liv halted, wishing she'd seen him first. "I wasn't, actually. I'm just browsing for books."

Stefan closed the hardback he was reading and laid it in his lap. "You've come to the right place. "There are over a hundred thousand volumes in this place, although most can't be found unless they want to be."

Liv laughed. "That's ridiculous. They're books, not Sophia."

"Books are exactly like your little sister," Stefan began. "They are compact treasures that appear ordinary, but once opened, reveal more magic and power than anyone thought could possibly be contained in such a small entity."

For a few long seconds, Liv studied Stefan, trying to gauge exactly what he might know about Sophia.

His laughter broke the tension building in her chest. "Of course, that's just my observation of the girl. I don't suppose I know much about her at all."

"No?" Liv posed.

"Well, I know that she lights up when you come around. That much is obvious. She has clearly missed having you around."

"Sophia never really knew me," Liv stated.

"Yet, you two get along like you had spent the last five years together." He held up the book he'd been reading. On the front cover in gold letters were the words, *Demons and Where They Hide*. "And to expand on what you were saying about books, I think they are very much alive. They have the power to spark ideas, breathe life into the nonexistent, and transport us to another realm. The books in this library happen to be a bit more outwardly cunning than those found in mortals' libraries, although even those volumes are full of power. These books just happen to know that they contain greatness and guard it from us, maybe waiting to decide if we're ready and worthy for the wisdom they offer."

Liv let out a long, loud yawn. "Do you often break into monologues? Because if so, I'll need to be warned before the next one."

Stefan set the book on the ottoman, his face unchanged. "Your cat also hides from you, if I remember correctly. The one you said was strangely in the House of Seven, although it is against the rules since he's an outsider."

"Most hide from me. It's sort of my thing," Liv said and

pointed to the book he'd laid down. "Are you trying to bring some demons out of hiding?"

Stefan's eyes cut to the volume and he actually smiled. "That was just a bit of light reading to get me ready for bed."

"Oh, don't you have a case to attend to? Like, innocent magicians who need your wrath or an elfin community you need to exert your influence over?"

"You're very skeptical of the House of Seven, aren't you? Why did you take on your responsibility as a Warrior if that was the case?"

"Maybe I'm hoping to be a part of the change."

Stefan sighed, looking around at the grand architecture of the library. "The House is due for changes, although I fear that implementing them will not be easy. For thousands of years, the House has operated the same way it always has. Some, like the Sinclairs, find this to be a point of great pride."

"I think it's a sign of stagnation," Liv shot back defiantly.

"I tend to agree with you." Stefan regarded her for a long moment, something apparently working in the recesses of his mind. Finally he said, "Is there a book I can help you find? Sometimes it's better to attack the collection in pairs. That makes it harder for the right book to get away."

Liv wanted to laugh, feeling like any venture in here was more of a safari than a casual bit of browsing in a library. "No, I don't think... Actually, what do you know about the creature who lives in the pond in the garden?"

From the expression that jumped to Stefan's face, this

wasn't a question he was expecting. "Creature? I think it's more accurately referred to as a monster, although I can't tell you what it is. It's tried to drown me at least once. Since then, I haven't risked getting that close."

Liv nodded. "Yeah, I made the same mistake when I was a child."

"You do have a flair for dabbling with things that are mysterious and dangerous, don't you?" Stefan asked.

The wall with the symbols seemed to be calling her. She wanted to try her ring on it, but the longer she hung around, the more questions Stefan asked her. She faked another yawn.

"Oh, it appears I've bored you," he said, bowing slightly. "I'll return to my book and leave you to your search." He sat back down on the sofa, pulling *Demons and Where They Hide* back onto his lap.

In her head, Liv quietly yelled, "Nooooo," wondering why he had stationed himself in the exact place she wanted to be. However, she kept the disappointment off her face as she waved to Stefan, leaving him alone in the one area of the library she desperately longed to search.

"I'll see you later," she said, striding in what she thought might be the direction of the exit.

"Yes, see you later, Liv."

CHAPTER TWENTY-ONE

The yawning darkness sought to eat Liv's courage as she hid under a large tree, watching the guard patrol the front of the Natural History Museum. She'd dismissed Rory's warnings, but alone in the dark, his words felt big enough to swallow her will.

Plato appeared beside her suddenly, the white tip of his tail standing out in the blackness of the night. "There are two guards inside the building."

Liv tried to nod, but she felt too stiff for even the simplest movement. "If I get myself in trouble, can you by any chance rescue me?"

The cat leapt, landing on the horizontal branch beside her. She hadn't even realized that the perch was there, and at such a perfect height. "There is nothing anyone can rescue you from that you can't get out of yourself."

"Oh good, more riddles."

Plato gave her an annoyed stare. "And you should know that if I can help, I will. However, I can't get the sword free."

"That's where the brownies come in," Liv stated.

"And I can't disable the security on the building," he continued.

"Yes, that's where I come in," she replied.

"Are you worried that you're not ready for this?" Plato asked.

"Are you?" she countered.

"I worry that you're putting yourself in danger for a giant's sword and a payoff that might not be worth the risk."

"Are you saying that I shouldn't do it?"

"If I did, would you turn around and go home?" Plato asked.

Liv shook her head. "Not a chance."

"Then stop stalling," Plato said. "Your opening is now."

The guard turned the corner of the building, disappearing out of her view. Liv didn't wait another second more before springing out of her hiding place and hurrying across the grounds. *The hardest part was the start,* she told herself. Now that she was in motion, the rest would go smoothly...she hoped.

High atop a nearby building, Stefan Ludwig watched as Liv Beaufont ran across the lawn and straight over to the side entrance to the Natural History Museum.

"What are you up to, Liv?" he mused.

Tracking her there hadn't been hard, which meant that he was going to have to teach her how to move through the city without being followed. If he'd been Adler or Decar

Liv would have been caught, and there would be no explanation that could get her out of trouble. Still, Stefan wondered what the magician was doing returning to the museum. He'd wanted to follow her before that night to find out what she did when not at the House of Seven, but an injury Hester had been unable to heal yet had prevented him from doing so. It had kept him away from a lot lately.

He lifted his arm and pulled up his sleeve, eyeing the bite in the moonlight. It was no worse than before but no better. Thankfully Hester had managed to stop the demon's poison before it did too much damage, but healing his arm completely was a different story. Maybe that was why he was there, watching Liv chant spells at the museum's security pad instead of off on his own mission.

Locating and slaying the demon who had done this to him wasn't going to be an easy feat, but Hester had assured him that it was the only way to heal the bite. She'd also promised him secrecy, at least for the moment.

Stefan had been assigned the case of hunting down some demons that were terrorizing mortals, and he'd mostly been successful. Slaying demons in this realm was one of his favorite pastimes. However, going into their lair and operating on their terms was a different story. He would do it, though. He'd assured Hester of that much, and she'd granted him the time. The last thing he needed was to worry his sister Raina, or for Adler or the others to doubt his strength as a Warrior.

Everything at the House of Seven was about perception. He'd learned that early on. And if they knew he'd been bitten while on a case, well, the level of difficulty of cases he was assigned would change. He'd seen it a hundred times. That was why Akio and Decar were given the hardest cases—because they were seen as the strongest Warriors. However, he suspected things were about to change. There was a new force in the House who was about to take them all by surprise. She didn't play by any of their rules, and apparently she worked her own cases on the side, Stefan noted as Liv slid into the museum undetected.

CHAPTER TWENTY-TWO

One of Liv's dreams was to break into a museum and have the entire place to herself. In that fantasy, she didn't have to jump up to see over the heads of strangers or wait in long lines. Or deal with slow walkers. Or really, deal with people at all.

Quiet excitement spilled over her as the security door released, and she stepped into the darkened corridor. Liv suddenly had the urge to run through the Natural History Museum, enjoying the freedom of having it all to herself.

A brisk shuffling noise startled her back to reality. She wasn't alone in here; it only felt like it. Two guards patrolled the floors every few minutes. That much Mortimer had been able to tell her after his brownies had done their reconnaissance. However, there were multiple other factors they didn't know as much about.

The guard strode by, not noticing Liv as she sank back against the wall. He whistled as he walked. *How stereotypical,* Liv thought, watching the back of his head as he swung a flashlight and sauntered towards the amphibian exhibit.

"Well, looks like I've got company tonight," the man said, his voice making Liv tense. *Had he seen her?* She peeked out from her place, the light from the corridor partially touching her head.

A woman carrying a box stood on the other side of the man, a forced smile on her face.

"Yes, we're updating the fetish carvings exhibit tonight," the woman who was the curator for that collection said, her eyes narrowing slightly.

Liv sunk back suddenly. *The woman had seen her!*

"What was that?" the curator asked, her voice a hoarse whisper.

"What was what?" the guard replied.

"Over there. By the side entrance. I saw something."

Damn it. Damn it. Damn it, Liv thought, her mind racing for an option. She could bolt out the door and escape, but then this mission would be over before it even started. The idea of failure hit Liv straight in the stomach, making her want to double over.

Instead, she took a page out of Sophia's book and melded herself into the wall. A flash of light hit her in the face, making her squint, but otherwise, she stayed as still as she possibly could, knowing that any movement would disrupt the illusion.

"Over here?" the guard asked. "I don't see anything."

"I could have sworn I saw someone looking around the corner," the woman stated.

"Well, maybe it was someone from your team," the man offered.

"Yeah, maybe," the curator replied, not sounding at all convinced.

The guard put the flashlight away, giving Liv a respite. "I'll do a few extra patrols tonight if it makes you feel better."

No, Liv thought. The plan was centered on the clockwork of the guard's schedules. Any change to that would throw everything off.

"I'd like that," the woman said. "Especially because my team will be in and out of the exhibit area throughout the night."

"Not a problem," the guard said, his footsteps fading as the two walked the other way. "Show me the exhibit you're working on."

"It's right over here."

Liv waited until their voices had died away to soft muttering before she peeled herself from the wall, the camouflage fading. She considered keeping up the glamour, but she didn't want to risk running through her magic reserves this early into the mission.

Sliding along the closest wall, Liv hurried to try to stay on schedule. If the guards would be patrolling more often, she had less time to get to the room with the sword than they'd planned. She hoped that the brownie who had come to help was fast.

When she was almost to the area where Turbinger lay, Liv froze. Her heart jumped into her throat. The exhibit they were updating on that night was directly next to the sword room.

Damn it, Liv thought, her brain cramping from the sudden complication. How was she supposed to stroll into that area and steal the sword with museum employees working right next to it?

Before, the mission had felt a little far-fetched, since they were relying on a brownie to open the case and remove the sword in less than six minutes. Now they had even less time, and more people to avoid. Well, *Liv* had to avoid them. The mortals apparently couldn't see brownies. It must be nice to be invisible, a spell Liv hadn't mastered. It would supposedly draw too much attention from the Council if she did use it.

"Are we going to get a dinner break?" a man called from the area with the fetish carvings.

"Of course," the woman from before replied. "Let's just get a few more things in place and then we can take a break."

That was going to be Liv's chance. However, there was another complication she had to worry about as she loitered in the corridor, hiding behind a large vase: the patrolling guards.

She had less than a minute before the next guard trotted around the corner behind her, spotting her position. Whipping her head back and forth, Liv waited until she heard his approaching footsteps and slipped into the recesses of the exhibit closest to her, hiding behind a life-sized zebra. Guilt pricked her throat when she realized that she was squatting directly on a protected museum exhibit, her back pressed against its fake shrubs.

When the patrolling guard had passed, Liv relaxed and stood up. It felt surreal to look out and see African animals all around her. She wondered why she hadn't chosen the elephant to hide behind. That would have been a bit better than trying to hide her whole body behind a zebra.

What has my life come to that this is even happening, Liv wondered with a silent laugh.

"Okay, this is the last box," the man working on the exhibit called, grunting as he set something down. "Can we go? The Thai place closes soon."

The woman sighed. "Yeah, go ahead."

"Aren't you coming?" another voice asked.

"Bring me back some yellow curry," the woman answered. "I've got too much work to do to leave here."

"Okay, we'll be back in half an hour."

Damn it, Liv exclaimed inwardly. Maybe she could turn the mortal into one of the fetish carvings and be done with it.

She reminded herself that the Council could be monitoring her magic use. If she was caught inside the museum and working with brownies, she was sure she'd be done in the House of Seven, which meant that the Beaufonts would be screwed. No, whatever happened, Liv had to play this carefully. This was about protecting her honor and her family's reputation...while also helping a giant.

Whistling echoed down the wide hallway. The other guard was back. They were coming around too often. Liv sank back down behind the zebra, waiting for him to pass. What she needed was a distraction; some way to pull these mortals away, if only for five minutes.

Just then something sparkled across the way, catching her eye.

CHAPTER TWENTY-THREE

On the far side of the museum, Liv caught the glint of gems and crystals sparkling in their cases. The thought that occurred to her next, simultaneously filling her with both hope and tension, was that she needed a distraction but not such a big one that the authorities would be called.

Making up her mind before she had a chance to over-think things, Liv stood up again, focusing on the exhibit across the way. It was at least twenty yards away, which meant that her aim had to be exact or she'd ruin her chances, along with a lot of precious gems.

With a clear intention, Liv directed her magic to the lights hanging over the gem exhibit. The overhead lights flickered, and the cases clicked as their security features were disabled. Using magic from this far away should have been difficult, but Liv had learned one very important lesson since having her magic unlocked: it reacted well to electronics.

SARAH NOFFKE & MICHAEL ANDERLE

"What's that?" the woman nearly yelled.

"It's coming from the gem exhibit," the guard answered, his voice suddenly tight. "Stay here, and I'll go check it out." He pulled his radio from his belt. "Tony, where are you? Can I get backup over at the gem exhibit?"

"I'm on my way," a voice radioed back.

"It looks like an electrical problem," the woman stated.

"That's typical. We've been having this problem lately. Stay here. I'll be back in a bit."

No, Liv thought. She'd hoped the distraction would take everyone away. She'd just have to resort to less primitive methods for the woman.

After the guard had sped off, Liv moved out of the African exhibit, trying to get a shot at the woman, whose back was thankfully to her as she unloaded small objects from a box. The incantation she muttered next was one she hadn't used in a very long time. She nearly laughed, thinking about how she and Clark used to use it on each other. Most siblings poked and pinched each other, but magicians could go to the next level of torture.

The woman stood suddenly. Tensed. Grabbed her midsection as she let out a small squeal of surprise. Then she promptly turned and strode toward the bathrooms located down the hallway. She moved quickly, probably trying to keep from peeing herself. It was a cruel trick, but it had done the job, and no one had gotten hurt.

When Clark and Liv had played the trick on each other, it had been common for one of them to accidentally wet themselves.

Feeling strangely amused and nostalgic, Liv hurried out

of her hiding spot while she had a chance. She soundlessly moved across the tile floor, sliding to a halt once she was in the room with Turbinger.

Her heart skipped a beat as she took in the scene before her.

CHAPTER TWENTY-FOUR

The sword was gone! How could it be gone? Where could it have gone? Liv looked around, expecting to see clues or scrapes or some other clue, but the room with its stark white walls didn't offer her anything.

The large case in the middle of the room looked peculiar sitting empty, only the indentions where the sword had laid evidence that Turbinger had been in the case.

Liv knew she was running out of time. The curator would be back from the restroom soon, and the guards would return. However, she didn't know where to go. She'd come for the sword, but it was gone. But where?

"Pssst," a small voice said by her feet.

Liv nearly jumped straight in the air, not having seen the small creature appear beside her. He was the same height as Mortimer but skinnier, his hair brushed to one side and trailing over his shoulder.

"Hey, were you sent by..." Liv's voice trailed away as she looked the brownie over, wondering if she could trust him.

He nodded. "My name is Freddy. And yes, Mortimer

sent me here to help you. However…" He pointed a long finger at the case. "The sword has been moved."

"What? By who?" she asked in a whisper.

He gave her a strange look. "By me, of course."

"Okay, but why? You were supposed to wait until I showed up."

"Yes, Ms. Liv Beaufont, Warrior of the House, but someone beat you to the sword, so I moved it before they could get it."

Liv blinked at the brownie. "I don't understand. Someone else came for the sword? Tonight?"

Freddy nodded, his body bobbing along with his head. "Thankfully I was here and noticed them approaching. That gave me enough time to get the sword out of its case and hide it."

Questions were streaming through Liv's head so fast she couldn't articulate them fast enough. "You moved the sword? But how? It's huge. And heavy. And who is this person who came for the sword?"

The brownie looked over his shoulder before returning his gaze to Liv, not looking as frantic as she felt. "I did move the sword. We can levitate things, which made it easy to move the sword, although I ran out of time to hide it properly, which is why you need to go and get it."

"Where did you put it?" Liv asked, a strange picture in her mind of the tiny brownie walking beside a huge hovering sword. It was important never to underestimate someone based on their size. They could still move great things.

"I put it in the room with the shiny rocks," Freddy squealed.

Liv nearly doubled over in defeat. "Are you serious? That was where I sent the guards so that I could get into this room."

Freddy nodded again, hopping forward as he did. "It's okay for now. I put it at the back of the exhibit. But the one who came after it will find the sword. They are already mad."

"Who is it?" Liv asked.

"An elf," Freddy answered. "One I've never seen before, who has a darkness in his eyes and a strange prowess that scares me."

"An elf?" Liv asked. "Like a regular-sized one?"

If this offended the brownie, he didn't show it. "Yes, and as you might have guessed, he could have gotten to the sword just as I did because the wards don't work on him. So I'm sorry, but I had to move it."

"You did good," Liv said, staring around and trying to figure out what she was going to do next.

"What exactly are you doing here?" the woman from before said at Liv's back.

CHAPTER TWENTY-FIVE

L iv almost rolled her eyes at the inopportune interruption. Before she had been worried about being caught by her. Now she found her a pest who was getting in the way of her fighting the mysterious villain lurking somewhere in the museum.

Slowly Liv turned around to face the woman, arranging her face into a neutral expression. "Hey. I'm here to work on the fetish carving exhibit. I think I'm lost, though."

"You're what?" the woman said, hesitation in her voice. Liv's statement didn't make sense to her, but she also didn't know enough to discount it. Liv could read this on the curator at once.

"I was added to the team at the last minute," Liv explained. "Where are we supposed to meet?"

The woman backed up, her eyes uncertain as she pointed. "Over here. Actually, I *could* use some more help—"

The lady's eyes widened in alarm as she halted and

revolved her chin to look in the direction of the case. The *empty* case.

"Where is the sword?"

Oh hell, Liv thought. *I can't catch a break today.*

Feigning surprise, Liv turned to look at the case too. Keeping this act up for very long wasn't going to work. Too bad for this woman that she was so observant. Liv was about to hit the woman with a spell when she staggered backward and slid down the wall, suddenly fast asleep.

Liv looked at her hand, wondering if her magic had poured out of her without her knowing it.

"That should keep her out for the rest of the night," Freddy said from beside Liv's knee.

"That was you? You did that?"

"Naturally."

"I didn't know that brownies could put mortals to sleep."

"How do you think we get our housework done?" he asked her, his hands on his hips.

"I thought you waited until they went to sleep."

"Nope. We put them to bed so we can do our chores."

Damn, I really *need to read that book Rory gave me,* Liv thought.

"What about the other mortals? They will be back soon," Liv said, peeking into the darkened corridor.

"I can take care of all of them," Freddy stated proudly. "The guards will be asleep before you even make it over to the fancy rock area." The elf disappeared, leaving Liv standing in front of the sleeping woman and staring at the small empty room.

She eyed the area outside the space. Somewhere in the

vast Natural History Museum was a deranged elf who was after Turbinger as well. It was hard to believe that she had thought the greatest obstacle that night would be stealing the sword from a mortal museum. Now it appeared that she was going to have to fight for Turbinger as well.

Once Liv had slunk into the gemstone exhibit, she realized that the security guards hadn't had a chance to fix the electrical problem she had created. The lights were still flickering overhead, and most of the cases appeared to be unlocked.

Liv nearly tripped over the guard who had been whistling before. He was sprawled on the floor, peacefully taking a nap as if he were curled up in his cozy bed and not on cold tile.

Freddy appeared to be a valuable ally, saving Liv from having to use her magic on the mortals or harm them in any way.

She lifted her hand to fix the lights she'd made malfunction when a creaking sound echoed through the exhibit. Liv spun, her hand extended and her eyes honing in on the figure lurking in the dark.

Standing beside an open case was a tall, slender man. He was attired in worn clothing such as one might see on a homeless person on the streets, but when he stepped out into the flickering light, Liv knew this was no mortal. The angle of his jaw and ears told her right away that he was an elf—and then there were those eyes. As Freddy had described, they were like two wells full of never-ending darkness.

"What do you want?" Liv asked, her hand still in the air.

"The same thing as you, Liv Beaufont," he answered, his voice like coarse sandpaper. "The question is, why do you want it?"

"Who are you?" Liv asked, stalling for time as she tried to figure out what her next move would be. She didn't know much about elves except that they were fast and powerful and drew from elemental power.

"I'm known by many names, but the question remains: why do you want Turbinger when it doesn't belong to you?"

"It doesn't belong to you either," Liv argued.

The elf tossed his long hair back as he laughed, showing a mouthful of yellow teeth. Suddenly she wanted to run and get as far away from this elf, who embodied evil. However, she reminded herself that she was a Warrior. This was not a challenge she could back down from, and there was no way she was losing her role over it.

"I've simply come to stop you from taking Turbinger," the elf said and reached into the case, his finger hovering inches from a beautiful purple crystal. He leeched power from it, and a moment later, the crystal's lush color faded to gray and it crumbled as if it were ash. In a flash, the elf directed his hand at Liv, sending a bolt of fire at her.

Liv's instincts took over and she ducked behind a nearby case. The fire vanished upon touching the glass as if it had been sucked into a vacuum.

Damn, this guy was out for blood.

Chancing a glance at the diabolical elf, Liv saw that he

was about to throw something in her direction again. She dove back to the ground, surprised again that the fire stopped before it reached her.

Something in the exhibit must be stopping his magic, she thought. He might be pulling from the elements, but they were just as strong at blocking him.

That was when she remembered what Freddy had said —that he'd hidden Turbinger at the back of this exhibit. She rolled over on her stomach, squinting towards the back wall, where more gems sparkled in the flickering light. Liv was starting to feel like she was in a strange club with a huge disco ball, the gems reflecting the lights and the blast of fire as the evil elf sought to torch her again.

Although she was safe behind this case of gems, her most important objective was getting to the sword. Well, and staying alive.

Liv took in a deep breath and bolted forward, keeping her head low, hoping to be unseen as she darted under the cases of gems towards the back.

The fire followed her, many of the attacks blasting her with heat, which meant that not all the cases had a protective quality to them.

When she had almost reached her objective, Liv was thrown on her back by a particularly strong hit. The air was knocked out of her and she coughed, trying to get her breath.

Damn, why couldn't I have fire magic? she wondered, trying to calm her lungs. It felt like they were on fire from breathing the strange greenish smoke lacing through the air.

That couldn't be good, she thought, trying to recall the

direction she had been going. It all looked the same now.

A particularly nasty ball of fire landed beside Liv, nearly blinding her for several moments. She shielded her eyes, backing away.

This running business wasn't doing her any good, and with each blast, she was getting more pissed. She wanted to stand up to this elf-jerk, but first she needed an edge. She needed Turbinger.

Liv dove when she saw the elf throw more fire in her direction. This asshole didn't care if he was destroying an exhibit. He was out for blood. The total disrespect for worldly treasures boiled Liv's blood, making her magic pour to the surface and beg to be released. Instead, she used it to speed to the back of the exhibit. When she thought she had another place to duck from the next attack, Liv came to a dead end.

This was it. She was trapped.

Liv turned around as the largest blast rocketed towards her like a meteor falling from the sky. Without even looking, Liv dove behind a large object, the force of the blast rolling her over several times. She pushed up to her hands and feet, blood trickling from her forehead. She'd been hit. All this running was making her lose her strength, and she had no idea how to fight an elf who had an endless supply of power in the form of precious stones and crystals.

Still rolling from the momentum, Liv's hand flew to the floor to try to stabilize her—and she felt it.

The cold metal. The power. The strength of something ancient. A raw and unyielding power. Liv looked down, the rubies from the sword winking at her from the hilt.

She was holding Turbinger.

CHAPTER TWENTY-SIX

Never before had Liv felt something so dangerously gorgeous. She was sure the energy radiating from the sword would take over her if she wasn't careful. However, everything was at stake for her, and the elf several yards away appeared to have nothing to lose. Liv made up her mind to let the sword control her and invited the power into her veins. At her core, she felt that it knew how to get them out of this.

It wasn't an object. She knew that instinctively. It had the feel of a person ten times her age and wisdom unmatched by anyone she'd ever met. It was the answer to all her problems, and might possibly be the cause of more if she wasn't careful.

Letting the rage of the sword purr through her, Liv sprang to her feet and lifted the sword over her head, the effort taking more than her strength. Magic fueled her as she swung the sword behind her head.

In front of her, a large stone stood on a stand, partially blocking her view. However, she still saw the elf's look of pure horror when she raised the sword. It sank down several inches like she didn't have the strength to keep it steady before it straightened again.

"I am Liv Beaufont, and if you want this sword, then you better come and take it from me," she yelled, her voice so loud it rattled the glass cases all over the exhibit. She didn't fear that they would shatter, but rather that she would live another day in this world unable to punish those who had betrayed her. It was at that moment that she realized those weren't *her* thoughts but rather the sword's. She knew that if she wasn't careful, Turbinger could take her over. It controlled people. Only someone very powerful was a match for it.

Although it took all her effort to keep the sword aloft, Liv knew she could manage Turbinger. Not for long, but she didn't need much time.

Bring my enemy to me, the sword directed in her mind. *I'll destroy him.*

How do you know I'm not your enemy? she dared to ask.

I know.

The elf sucked the energy from another gem, making it turn black and crumble to dust in the open case. He hurled a streak of fire at Liv, but unlike before, she didn't dodge as it soared toward her. Instead, her eyes stayed pinned to it, her fingers tensed on the hilt of the sword.

She didn't even feel in control as she waited until the last possible moment, swinging the sword around to combat the fire, knocking it back to where it had originated like a baseball player hitting a home run.

The elf realized a moment too late what had happened.

The fire knocked him to the ground, flames and smoke erupting around him.

Go!

As if she had been pushed, Liv charged toward the elf with the sword in her hand. She felt the rage of a hundred wars pouring through her veins, and vengeance thick on her tongue. Liv tasted every battle the sword had ever been in, which was both exhilarating and scary. She wanted to throw the sword down, but it was melded to her hands, unrelenting.

Everything was a blur until she found herself standing over the elf, who was cringing, his hands covering his face as he rolled back and forth, trying to extinguish his own fire.

"What you seek to burn will scorch you from the inside out," Liv said, but the words weren't her own. She didn't even know where they'd come from. "This feud is soon to be over. The power will shift. Tell them."

The elf scooted to his rear end, pushing himself backward as Liv swung the giant's sword to the left and right in a fluid motion.

"They will kill me if I return without it," the elf yelled, his voice tearful. He reached out. "You might as well murder me."

Turbinger wanted to. Liv felt the bitter yearning from the sword to slice through the elf before them, a force she felt powerless to control. However, from somewhere in the depths of her soul, she rallied a strength she didn't even know she had. As the sword swung around, possessed by its own desire, Liv wrestled it down. The blade sliced the elf's extended arm, the one he had stretched out to beg for mercy in the form of death.

The elf jerked back holding his bleeding arm, shock and disappointment on his face. Liv held the sword down by her side even though it was fighting her grip, trying to be swung again.

"Go! Run! Get out of here. I never want to see you again!" Liv yelled, straining against the sword's simmering power.

"But you don't understand. They will hunt me down," the elf said, cradling his arm.

"Who? Who do you work for?"

The elf looked at the sword, which had started to glow as if the anger within it was seeping out. It jerked in Liv's grasp, and she knew that soon she wouldn't be able to control its power. Turbinger would break free.

"Go!" Liv yelled.

The elf, needing no more encouragement, sprinted from the room, leaving Liv exhausted and holding what she believed to be the deadliest weapon in the world.

CHAPTER TWENTY-SEVEN

The gem room had been destroyed. Liv didn't know how she could repair it so that no one noticed what had happened. Although she'd put out the fires, the scorch marks and smell of smoke gave away that a battle had happened there. And the gems. How was she going to replace the ones the elf had turned to ash? It had never been her plan to destroy part of the museum to get the sword, although in the morning, the Natural History Museum would know it had been stolen. The cameras wouldn't tell them anything since they'd been disabled from the start, but the gem room? She had to fix it.

With the battle over, it was harder to carry Turbinger, which was nearly as tall as she was and weighed much more than she did. She dragged it back in the direction she'd come, looking for Freddy.

She found the brownie arranging carvings in the exhibit next to the sword room. Propped against the wall and sleeping peacefully were the museum curator and three men.

Freddy turned as she approached, polishing one of the stone fetish carvings with a thoughtful look on his face. "I see you were successful," he said, glancing at the sword that was now resting on her shoulder, its weight pinching her skin.

"I got Turbinger, so for that I'm grateful," she said, finding she was suddenly out of breath.

"You sound disappointed," Freddy observed, placing the carving on a glass shelf and retrieving another from a nearby box.

"The gem exhibit has been sort of destroyed," Liv admitted.

"And the elf?"

Liv brought the sword down, its tip resting on the floor, her hands on the hilt. The elf's blood marked the blade, reminding her that she'd nearly killed him. Well, Turbinger had. "I let him go."

The brownie lifted an eyebrow, his hollow eyes full of curiosity. "That is a strange thing for a magician to do. He was your enemy."

Liv shook her head. "I don't know who he was or who sent him. But no, I don't think he was my enemy. Only a pawn."

Freddy nodded, turning back to the shelf to arrange the carvings. "And you got what you came here for, which is all that matters."

"It's *not* all that matters," Liv said, feeling the weight of everything that had happened in the last hour pressing on her shoulders. "The way we do things is almost more important than the things we do."

"Those are wise words," the brownie said absentmindedly.

"My father used to say that," Liv admitted, looking fondly at the mortals sleeping peacefully. She wished for a moment that she could be them, dreaming without a care in the world.

"I can fix the gem room," Freddie said.

Liv's chin jerked back in the brownie's direction. "You can? How?"

"Well, I can't replace anything that was lost, but I can clean it up so it doesn't appear that a battle happened there."

"Really? That would be fantastic!" Liv said, her chest lightening suddenly. "Thank you. And I guess a dozen gems missing in a collection of a few thousand will be okay. The museum will just think that whoever stole the sword also took those."

"The authorities will be very curious about what happened on this night," Freddie stated, a giggle in his voice.

"And the mortals?" Liv gestured in their direction. "What will they think?"

"They will awake not remembering anything and find their work all done," Freddie explained, hopping down from the stool he'd been standing on. "I've wiped their memories since I didn't want you to have to do it."

A smile cracked Liv's face. "Thank you. That was very thoughtful. The Council—"

"—shall not know." Freddie finished her sentence. "Mortimer said you and he keep secrets from the Council. This will be one of them."

"Wow, you really saved my butt tonight. I appreciate

everything. If you hadn't gotten to the sword first and hidden it, the elf would have it."

Freddy picked up packing materials, folding them and laying them back in the boxes, taking great care with every action. He worked proudly and as if each task consumed his full attention. "I have never worked for a magician before. However, I've liked helping you tonight. You are different, Liv Beaufont, Warrior of the House of Seven."

"Tell me about it," Liv wise-craked. "I'm considered sort of uncooperative, and there is probably a whole list of names the Councilors call me behind my back."

"The things people say behind your back are never worth your time," Freddie told her as he worked. He looked up at her, a meaningful expression in his eyes. Liv noticed how old and wise he appeared. "Mortimer wanted me to give you this if I so desired." He turned over his hand to reveal a small envelope sealed with wax and a symbol she supposed represented the brownies.

"If you so desired?" Liv hesitated, not grabbing the letter although she wanted to.

"True character is revealed in battles," Freddie stated. "When a warrior is faced with life and death, taking or giving, preserving or destroying, their real self comes out. Mortimer doubted that his loyalty in you was well-placed, but I think you have put his fears to rest tonight. I will communicate that to him, ensuring that the brownies are forever your servants."

Liv's mouth fell open. She didn't know what to say, which might have been a first.

Freddy extended his hand, urging her to take the envelope. "You asked Mortimer for information on a canister of magic. I think he's found clues for you, but I know no more than this. The letter will explain the rest."

Her heart pounding with excitement, Liv reached for the letter. "Thank you. This is wonderful. I rescued the sword, and now this!"

Freddy nodded good-naturally, returning to his work organizing the carvings.

Liv slipped the letter into her cape and lifted the sword to her shoulder again. "I should get out of here, but I can help if you need me to."

Freddy shook his head as he pulled out a rag to polish the carving he was working on. "I work better alone. All brownies do. And like I said, from this point forward, we are your servants. You have important business to attend to and should be off."

"But you don't have to be my servants," Liv argued. "I never asked for it. And really, I think what the brownies and I have should be considered a mutual partnership."

Freddy turned to face her, a strange smile making the many wrinkles on his face deepen. "You are exactly right. We don't have to be your servants, and working for a magician is a first as far as I know. Brownies choose who they work for. We take great care deciding that. And if you'd rather call it a partnership, that's up to you, although I don't think it should really matter. The reality is that if you ever need us, all you must do is ask and we will be there to serve."

Liv bowed her head in gratitude. "The reason I insist we call it a partnership is that the same is true of the brownies. If you ever need anything from me, I'll be there to help as well."

CHAPTER TWENTY-EIGHT

Multiple times, Stefan had wanted to abandon his hiding place on the roof of the neighboring building and rush into the Natural History Museum to help Liv. However, he wasn't sure that she'd see it as a good thing. And in truth, he wasn't sure she needed his assistance. He just wanted to help, but his curiosity was getting the better of him. For a solid hour he watched the museum, seeing nothing but a few mortals leaving and returning with takeout and an elf hurrying away. Then he spotted streaks of fire inside the museum through the exterior glass walls. Something incredible was happening in there, and he was desperate to know what it was.

When Liv finally exited the museum, Stefan could hardly make out her form, as if she'd disguised it somehow. She was carrying something large, but from that distance, it was impossible to know what it was. He reasoned that if she'd used magic to disguise it, it might be impossible to tell what it was except up close.

He'd just have to get a closer look and find out where she was going. He was certain it wasn't the House of Seven.

Stefan took three steps and leapt off the two-story building, landing gracefully on the ground below, never losing sight of Liv. However, when he went to take his next step, his feet were strangely stuck to the ground. He nearly fell to his hands and knees from the effort of trying to dislodge them. No spell that he tried unsealed his feet from the pavement. It didn't make any sense. What sort of spell had been used on him? And when?

Jerking his head up as he pulled at his feet, Stefan watched as Liv disappeared down an alley, getting away from him. Following her was out of the question now. He'd never be able to catch up. She'd probably create a portal and disappear before he'd even crossed the street.

As if the seal had been broken by his disappointment, Stefan's boots came free. His sudden momentum carried him several feet before he turned around to eye the place he'd been stuck. There were no markings on the sidewalk or any other clue why he'd been trapped there. However, as he continued to study the area, he noticed a cat sitting next to the building he'd been stationed atop. It was mostly white, with large black spots. When the feline stretched to a standing position, his tail, which was black save for the white tip, went up into the air.

Stefan didn't think he imagined the smug look the cat gave him as it sauntered around the building and out of sight.

CHAPTER TWENTY-NINE

C loaking the sword had been Plato's idea, and it had been a good one. Otherwise, Liv didn't know how she would have looked walking through the streets of Los Angeles carrying a giant's sword.

Putting a cloak on Turbinger hadn't been easy, though. The sword, whose personality she was learning more about each moment she spent with it, didn't want to be concealed. Finally, after explaining to the sword the importance of the cloak, it allowed the magic, hiding it from the view of passersby. Thankfully no one saw her leaving the museum, or when she stepped out of the portal onto Rory's street. If they had, she would have looked like she was carrying a cello.

It was after midnight when she hauled the sword to Rory's door. Not only would she be grateful to not have to carry Turbinger around anymore, but she'd also enjoy having her head back. While she held the sword, she heard its wants and thoughts and felt its memories. It wanted justice, a desire she could relate to. The sword thought of nothing but its masters throughout the centuries, and its memories were full of blood and battles and a pain unlike no other she'd ever experienced.

The lights in Rory's house were off when she dragged the sword to the door. She'd never seen the house like this. Even at night, the lights from inside spilled out through the windows, casting the yards in brightness as if a full moon shone overhead.

Keeping two hands on Turbinger, Liv kicked the door.

No one answered.

Again she kicked at the door, almost expecting it to swing open like it usually did when she arrived. However, it appeared that the house's occupant was asleep and hard to wake.

Liv kicked the door even harder, making a barrage of noise. She made a note that she'd have to wipe her footprints from its surface before she left.

"What do you want?" Rory yelled as he opened the door, confused outrage on his face. Kittens spilled from behind the door and tumbled over Liv's feet, taking this opportunity to play. Rory's eyes were red, and his face was partially covered by his messy hair. He pushed it out of his face, and his expression changed to one of pure disbelief.

"No!" He gasped. "Y-y-you did it."

Liv offered him a confident smile. "You doubted me?"

"No, I just figured…" Rory reached for Turbinger but pulled back like he was afraid. "I thought it might take time. I didn't expect…"

"I sort of think we should have a ceremony, but you're not dressed for it and I'm tuckered out. What *are* you wearing, by the way?"

Rory came back to reality, dragging his eyes away from the sword long enough to look down at the dressing gown he was wearing. The sleeves were tied around his wrists with bows, and the bottom was trimmed with lace. "It's my sleep shirt."

"It's a tent, and it has lace on it," Liv stated.

"Here, come in." Rory stepped back, waving her into his mostly dark house. The kittens followed, and when the door had closed, a flame erupted in the fireplace, offering just enough light.

Liv strained as she put her hand under the blade and lifted Turbinger so it was horizontal. "Rory, are you ready to take your grandfather's sword, or would you like to put on pants first?"

He simply nodded, his eyes not wavering from the sword.

"Is that a yes about taking Turbinger or about putting on pants?" she joked, extending her arms, which shook from the fatigue of holding the weapon.

"I-I-I don't know if I'm ready..." Rory backed up a step.

Liv dropped her chin to her chest. "Are you serious? I nearly got all my hair burned off getting you this sword. And it's a beast, so be warned. You don't get to turn into a psychopath after taking hold of this thing."

Combing his hand through his hair, Rory gawked at her. "I can't believe you got it. I never expected..."

"Yes, we've established how little faith you had in my ability to complete this mission," Liv told him, again holding the sword out a few inches. "Take Turbinger, Rory. It's you it belongs to."

With shaking hands, Rory reached out, his eyes buzzing

with excitement. When he wrapped his hands around the hilt, he lifted the sword like it weighed nothing, holding it with practiced grace in front of him.

His eyes widened, and Liv knew exactly why. It was the voice of Turbinger running through his head. The images. The feelings. The unrelenting energy it possessed.

"Wow, I knew it was powerful, but I had no idea *how* powerful," Rory exclaimed, closing his eyes and listening.

"The sword isn't just powerful, it's dangerous," Liv informed him, "which is why I'm confident that if anyone should have it, it should be you. Someone needs to protect this weapon from whoever else wants it." Liv began telling Rory the story of the elf at the Natural History Museum. He tested the balance of the sword many times as she told him what had happened. When she was done, he gave her an earnest look.

"I'm sorry that I put you in that kind of danger. I didn't know others would be going after the sword."

"Well, I don't think they were," Liv stated. "I think I triggered their attention when I first tried to get Turbinger."

"Then maybe they didn't want the sword for themselves," Rory reasoned. "It's been there for decades, and no one has tried to take it. Maybe they only didn't want you to steal it and give it back to the giants."

"But then there's the question of why? Why did someone put the sword there in the first place, surrounding it with magical wards that kept you out? Why did they want to keep it away from the giants?"

"There is a lot of history that I don't know," Rory admitted. "And there's even more I choose to ignore, although my ancestors didn't. Magicians and giants, as you know, haven't gotten along for centuries."

"I think there's a way to fill in the missing pieces," Liv said, looking at the sword in Rory's hands.

He seemed to understand immediately, his eyes following hers. "It has a story to share."

She nodded. "And hopefully, it will tell it in time. When it does, will you share?"

He thought for a moment and then agreed. "Yes, I will tell you what I learn from Turbinger."

Junebug had been trying to get Liv's attention since she'd entered. She leaned over and picked up the hairball, cradling him. He was having none of that and climbed onto her shoulder, where he perched, watching Rory admire the sword.

After a moment, he looked at her like he'd forgotten she was still there watching him. "I don't have your sword ready."

"Because you didn't expect me to fulfill my end of the deal," Liv teased.

"Because crafting a sword takes time," he corrected. "It won't take much longer, though."

"Just don't make it as big as that mammoth one. I'm going to need a massage after lugging that thing around."

Rory chuckled, something he did so rarely that it always got her attention. "It was pretty funny to see you holding this when I opened the door."

She joined him, imagining the sight in her head. "Yeah, I bet you not only didn't expect me to get the sword but also didn't think I could carry it back to you."

Rory's smile vanished. "I never doubted your ability to

retrieve Turbinger. I only expected that it would take longer. And I knew you'd find a way to deliver it to me, although it is as big as you."

It felt like they were on the edge of a moment...so Liv went to the front of the house. "Sorry I kicked your door to get your attention. That thing requires both hands."

He didn't look concerned as he set the sword into a holder above the fireplace. Liv hadn't noticed it was there, but it seemed to be made for the sword.

"Wasn't there a painting in that spot before?" Liv asked.

"There was," Rory said, stepping back and admiring Turbinger shining in the firelight. He turned to face her, exhaustion edging his features. "I'll have your sword ready in a week, or maybe less. And no, it won't be this big. I've made it for you, based on your size."

"So it will be more like a dagger?" Liv joked.

Rory rolled his eyes. "It will be a sword."

"Hey, in the meantime, if you want to teach me how to create fireballs, I'd appreciate it. So damn tired of getting flames thrown at me."

"That's gnome and elf magic," Rory said. "I can make you a sword and teach you how to stay alive. Well, if you can learn to keep your mouth shut."

"So I'm doomed, then?"

Rory flicked his hand at the door and it opened, a hint that it was time for her to leave. "I'll see you tomorrow, Liv, and we'll look at adding combat magic to your arsenal."

Liv pulled Junebug off her shoulder and set him on the floor. He and the other kittens took off for the back of the house, sounding like a herd of cows. "Yeah, there won't always be a giant's sword lying in the perfect place to save my ass."

When she was at the door, Liv turned around. Rory's gaze was glued on the sword, the disbelief back.

"All right, good night. I'll see you tomorrow."

"Yeah," Rory said absently, lost in thought.

When she'd crossed the threshold, Rory let out a heavy sigh. "Hey, Liv?"

She looked over her shoulder at him.

"Thank you for returning Turbinger home. It's not my grandfather, but it's as close as I'll ever get, and that means...well, more than you could know."

Liv glanced at the sword hanging over the fireplace, a sharp prickle spreading through her chest. "Oh, I think I understand. Just remember, *familia est sempiternurn*."

Rory nodded, a tender expression on his face. "Yes, family *is* forever."

CHAPTER THIRTY

Staring at the box on the counter, Liv stood motionless. "Well, it's not going to make itself," Plato said, jumping up on the counter and rubbing his face against the cardboard corner.

"I thought that was how magic worked?" Liv joked.

"And I thought you were trying to learn how to do things without magic before coasting through the rest of your life relying on spells."

Liv raised an eyebrow at the cat. "I didn't realize you had such a strong opinion about magic."

"I just think it's important not to become overly dependent on it," Plato explained. "The best magicians I've known could get themselves out of a dire situation without their magic, but had the upper hand when they employed it along with their practical skills."

Liv let out a sigh and opened the box. "Fine. I'll learn how to cook."

"The meal kit has all the ingredients and instructions. How hard can it be?" Plato asked.

"Says the cat who doesn't have opposable thumbs."

A knock on the door made Liv jump. She had been extra-tense since the museum, expecting the authorities to show up and arrest her for the robbery. The news channels had broadcast many reports about the break-in, all offering zero information on suspects or leads the police were pursuing.

Liv let out a sigh after looking through the peephole. Of course he was early, she thought. That had always been his style.

She opened the door and ushered Clark into her apartment. "Get in here. Did anyone see you?"

He looked over his shoulder. "No. I'm careful not to be followed or seen, unlike someone at the Natural History Museum. I still can't believe you blew out the windows and jumped off the roof."

"What can I say? I get inspired by culture and art."

Clark pursed his lips and scratched his nose. "You wouldn't by chance have been involved with the recent theft there?"

Liv held her arms out wide. "Do I look big enough to carry that giant sword that was stolen?"

"Liv!" Clark said, his voice full of tension.

She waved him off. "What's the Council saying about the incident?"

He rolled his shoulders and sighed. "That's the thing. Adler is acting like it isn't our business, telling us we should focus on other cases."

"Sounds like he doesn't think magic was involved," Liv said hopefully.

"Well, no magic that corresponds to the event came up

on the radar from registered magicians, but I'm still unsure. How did you do it?"

He asked the last question so casually that Liv gave him props. She smiled. "Nice try, but that's not why I asked you to come over."

"I thought we were going to be open and honest with each other?" Clark said, his tone stern.

Liv's attempt at lightness was instantly squashed by his seriousness. He was right. "Well, I think the less you know about this, the better, but it *could* be related to what we're working on." As she unpacked the ingredients from the box of food, Liv explained what she was doing. She couldn't help but laugh when Clark flinched every time she mentioned Rory.

He began to pace as she started making baked ziti.

"You're working with a giant?" he nearly yelled, his face flushing pink. "Why didn't you tell me?"

"Because for some strange reason, I thought you'd over-react," she said, stirring the pasta and rereading the directions.

"Overreact? Of course I would. They can't be trusted. Do you know what they've done to magicians?"

"I actually don't. Do you know? Why can't they be trusted?"

"Well, they...they...they refuse to have their magic registered with the House."

"Which makes them different from other magical creatures how?"

Clark halted, momentarily thrown off. "Well, it's the same as them. But they are different because..."

"Because?" she prompted when he didn't continue.

"Liv, it's different with giants."

"That's just the thing, Clark—I don't think it is. We've been fed certain information our whole lives, you more than me, but it doesn't add up. Why is there a dispute? Why was the giant's sword put into the mortals' museum? Who put magical wards around it?"

He pointed behind her. "I don't know, but your water is boiling. What are you doing, anyway?"

"I'm cooking you dinner," she said proudly.

Clark's chin tucked back on his neck. "Why would you do that?"

She shrugged, stirring the water and gesturing at Plato. "I don't know. The cat said I should." Liv rummaged through her drawer for a can opener for the crushed tomatoes, but she couldn't find one. She winked at Plato. "Turn your head. I'm going to use magic to open this can, but in my defense, I already know how to open cans."

He set his head down on his paws, not looking like he cared in the least.

"You know that restaurants make food?" Clark said. "Actually, the House's chef, Mario, makes incredible dishes."

"I remember," Liv agreed. "But in all seriousness, I'm trying to learn how to do things without using magic."

"I don't understand. You had your magic locked for five years. Why didn't you learn how to do these things then?"

Liv strained the pasta, waving the steam out of her face. "I was learning other things, like how to repair flat irons and fix hair dryers." What she didn't say was that she had been trying to figure out how to fix herself, but it hadn't worked. She had been trying to learn how to survive during the last five years. Now she was looking forward to figuring out how to thrive.

"What's a flat iron?" Clark asked.

"It's science. You wouldn't understand."

He shrugged. "Yeah, probably not."

"Anyway, I know you don't approve of me hanging out with giants and breaking into museums, but—"

"That's just the thing! The more you make your case, the more I get it. Just like the canister of magic, I'm starting to see that there's a lot I don't understand that doesn't make sense. There is definitely something going on."

Liv's eyes sparkled as she pulled the still-sealed envelope from her jeans. "Speaking of the canister, I might have some information."

"You didn't open this?" Clark asked after she told him the story about the brownies and what they'd offered her. He ran his finger over the seal on the envelope, his gaze intense.

"I wanted to wait for you," Liv explained. "We're in this together."

Clark gazed at her, a thoughtful expression on his face. "Thanks. This proves it." He handed her the letter. "Open it."

She took the envelope and ran her finger under the seal, breaking the wax. On the front of the card were two words: Zietgort Monastery.

Liv didn't know what she had expected the note to say, but that definitely wasn't even close.

"Is that where the canister of magic is?" Clark asked, taking the note and turning it over as if looking for more.

"I guess so. But why would Adler or whoever it was put the canister there?"

"Maybe it's being used by someone there," Clark offered.

The timer in the kitchen sounded, pulling their attention away from the letter that offered too little information and yet more than they could have hoped for.

"None of this makes any sense. I recovered the canister of magic and brought it to the House of Seven, and then it disappears, as well as any records of it. Now it's located in a monastery." Liv pulled the baked ziti out of the oven. It was perfectly browned on the top, with steam rising from the center. Clark had told her she'd put too much cheese in it, but that had only prompted her to dump another handful into the dish.

"We've got to go there and find out more," Clark said, watching as Liv piled two large scoops onto a plate and handed it to him. "This is too much for me."

"No, it's not, because it's the best thing you've ever eaten and you're going to eat all of it and then want seconds, but I will shut you down since I'm eating all of the rest of this," she said, waving to the casserole dish filled with baked ziti. "And I agree about going to this monastery, but there is no 'we' about it. I'm going by myself."

Clark put down his fork and regarded her with a disappointed look. "What happened to working together?"

"We are, but we don't have to be sloppy," Liv said,

blowing on her bite. "If we're caught together, we're screwed. However, if *I'm* caught, you can plead innocence."

Clark considered this for a moment. "Yeah, I guess you're right. Hopefully you won't be discovered by the House of Seven, but if you are, you can just make up some excuse like you did with the museum. I think the Council is starting to expect you to do random weird stuff." He set down his fork again, a look of surprise jumping to his face. "Hey, you started working with the brownies. Does that mean you didn't enforce the new regulations on them?"

Liv took a bite, the warmth and creaminess filling her mouth. "Of course not. I'm not even working the current case they gave me. I'm just going to let a few more days go by and tell them I completed it."

Clark shook his head. "That's not going to work for long. We'll figure it out."

"No, the Council won't, because they are only assigning me dumb cases to keep me out of their hair."

"That's completely true," Clark stated, finally taking a bite. His eyes widened as he chewed. "Wow, this is actually pretty good."

Liv rolled her eyes at him. "Of course, it is. You can't even taste the poison I put in it."

"Ha-ha. I watched you make the entire dish." Clark shoveled another bite into his mouth, bigger than the last.

"Good. That means that you know how to do it and can make it for me next time."

"I don't think so, Liv. Doing things without magic might be your thing, but it isn't mine," Clark stated, pointing at the casserole dish with the leftovers. "You're not going to eat all that. I say we split it when I'm done with this."

"And I say you fight me for it," Liv countered with a wink. "I need to practice my combat magic."

"Fine," Clark agreed, taking the last bite from his plate. "But get ready to pee yourself."

CHAPTER THIRTY-ONE

"I'll see you later, John," Liv called from the back of the shop.

"Not if I see you first," he replied, ducking his head through the door to the front and smiling widely.

"Oh, you and your dad jokes. Don't forget to eat a vegetable today. And take your medication."

He held up the donut he was working on. "Does this count? It was fried in corn oil."

"No. Eat a carrot."

John grimaced. "No, thanks."

"I'm bringing you some carrot cake tomorrow." With that parting shot, Liv and Plato exited through the back. The sun was just setting, casting the alley in shadows. She pulled her hood up over her head and began striding away from the store's door. After some practice, Liv had found the perfect place to open a portal from the back area that couldn't be seen from the road. That ensured she didn't have to go all the way home to use portal magic, which was making commuting much easier.

"Liv…" Plato began, his voice tentative.

She halted, knowing exactly what he was referring to without him saying it. "Yeah, I know what you mean."

Spinning around, Liv lifted her hand, releasing a disarming spell. Thanks to her sparring match with Clark, she'd mastered it. He'd also taught her how to use fire magic, although she still needed a flame present to do it.

Stefan appeared, seemingly out of nowhere, stumbling backward into the dumpster. He caught himself, a fierce look on his face.

"This is considered stalking." Liv crossed her arms over her chest with a determined expression. "Why are you following me…again?"

Stefan's eyes bounced between her and Plato. "And here I thought you didn't know I was trailing you. I was going to offer you tips on how to move around without being followed."

"I prefer to allow others to think I'm oblivious. Being underestimated is one of my key strategies when facing an opponent."

"I'm not your enemy," Stefan said, brushing off his leather jacket and coming a few steps closer.

"Why are you following me, then? Does the Council want you to babysit me?"

He shook his head. "No, I'm doing this on my own. I know you're working on something besides your Warrior cases."

Liv held her hand out, indicating the shop. "Yes, I work here fixing appliances. Do you have an electric razor or a toaster you want me to fix?"

Stefan hazarded a smile that lit up his blue eyes. "No, I use magic for those things."

She shook her head and clicked her tongue, looking down at Plato. "All these magicians who rely on magic for everything. If it was taken away from them tomorrow, they'd be helpless."

Stefan nodded in the direction of the cat. "And this must be the cat who can enter the House of Seven uninvited."

"Are you going to tattle on me? Adler is looking for any reason to put me in timeout or whatever they do to punish uncooperative Warriors."

"Liv, I'm not following you because I want to get you in trouble. I wouldn't tell Adler or the other Councilors a damn thing about you. I have a feeling that you and I could be working together, but I need to know what you're up to. Like why you broke into the Natural History Museum, and why you stole that sword."

"What? A sword was stolen?" Liv feigned surprise. "I was there for a late study group. We're putting together a really rad insect collection."

"Fine, I get that you don't trust me, and I understand why. Lots of shifty things happen at the House of Seven, but I'm not like Adler or his minions. Raina and I are working to restore balance to the House."

"How?" Liv challenged.

"Well, for one, I don't hunt down and dispose of magicians who aren't registered. I warn them. Give them ways to hide."

"Why would you do that?"

"Because killing our own is wrong. Killing the innocent

is wrong, and it was never the House's right to own a magician's magic. That's not how justice works."

Liv didn't want to admit it, but Stefan sounded a lot like her. For that reason, she was even warier of him. Someone trying to get her trust would say exactly what she wanted to hear.

"I work alone," Liv said after a moment of deliberation.

"It appears that you work with the lynx." Stefan motioned to Plato.

"That's because I know I can trust Plato. I don't know a thing about you."

Stefan gave her an amused look. "You named your cat after a philosopher?"

"I didn't name him."

Plato twitched his tail in irritation. "I'm tired of people thinking I was named after him when it was the other way around."

Liv took a step back. "I'm going to open a portal and leave. You're not going to follow me anymore. If you want me to trust you, stop stalking me. Tell me what you know about the House and share information with me, then we'll see what happens."

Stefan nodded. "Fine, that's fair enough. But if I need my television fixed, can I come by the shop again?"

Liv turned around, putting her back to the warrior. "No. And you shouldn't be watching television. Go work your cases, already."

She opened a portal and disappeared, Plato following her.

CHAPTER THIRTY-TWO

After portaling three more times, Liv was certain Stefan wasn't following her. "What are your thoughts on him?" she asked Plato as they hiked up the lush green hill on top of which the monastery was situated. It was an old stone building with three tall towers that rose high into the pristine blue sky.

"I think he's hiding something," Plato said, aware she was referring to Stefan even though they hadn't spoken for ten minutes.

"Like that he's behind whatever is going on with the House?"

"I don't think so. My instinct tells me he isn't lying about letting off unregistered magicians. Still, I think it's dangerous to trust anyone but Clark with what you're investigating."

Liv agreed with a nod. Ian's and Reese's deaths were still a mystery. So were her parents'. Maybe they'd gotten too close to the truth, but someone would have to know that, and that person could be anyone. No, it wasn't smart for her to build bridges with Stefan. Not until he had proven he could be trusted.

"Do I ring the doorbell?" Liv asked when they made it to the large door at the front of the monastery.

"I think you knock," Plato told her, nodding in the direction of the large knocker on the door.

Liv had considered breaking into the monastery to investigate, but that felt wrong, considering what it was. She might not be a religious person, but she respected the sanctity of other people's religions.

The knock echoed through the grounds, sending a sudden chill over her arms. If she were caught there by someone from the House, she didn't know what she'd say. Clark had said she could plead ignorance, but that would only work for so long.

A man dressed in long brown robes pulled the door open, his expression uncertain. After taking one look at Liv, he turned and strode into the monastery. "Follow me," he said, walking away with a slight limp.

Liv was unsurprised to discover that Plato had disappeared. She sped up to catch the old man, which wasn't hard. "Hello, my name is—"

"I know who you are, my child, and I'm taking you to what you seek."

Liv tilted her chin to the side, trying to decide what she should say to that. She had this whole fake story lined up, but it appeared that today she didn't get to be Ethel Notterbottom—which was slightly disappointing.

"How do you know who I am?" she finally asked, smiling at monks as she strode by some who had gathered in the courtyard.

"I just know," the man answered. "I am Niall, and I have been taking those from the House of Seven to this location for as long as I can remember, although I can never remember who I take or why." He shrugged his bony shoulders. "It's not my responsibility to know, though. I'm a simple servant."

This didn't make any sense. The canister was in this monastery, but House members came here to find something. What was it?

"We're going down now," Niall said, grabbing a lantern by a set of stairs and descending into darkness.

Liv tensed at the top of the stairs, trying to decide if she should follow. The monk seemed harmless; it was more about what might be waiting for her in the dark tunnel. She'd come this far, though and reasoned that she couldn't turn back now.

"You don't remember who from the House comes here?" Liv asked.

"I don't remember many things about these trips," Niall said.

Memory charms had obviously been used on the monk, and as Liv strode through the damp tunnels, she realized that there was one at work on her too. She had no idea where they were and had an inherent feeling of being lost.

After they took several turns, Liv felt she was in a maze and could never find her way to her destination alone. Getting out, however, didn't seem hard. Just considering the idea made her feel that she'd be instantly spat out of the area if she so desired. This was a strange magic, one she had never heard of.

Niall stopped without notice and held up the lantern. "What you seek is there. I'll wait for you if you like."

Liv looked down to where the tunnel dead-ended, a shudder tickling her core. "You should go. I don't want to keep you."

The monk nodded. "Very well. Until next time." He turned, limping back the way they'd come, the lantern light making the edges of his figure glow slightly.

Liv opened her palm and summoned a light, but nothing happened.

"Your magic doesn't work here," Plato said, appearing beside Liv, the white tip of his tail standing out in the dark.

Liv rolled her eyes and pulled a flashlight from her pocket. "I bet you're screaming, 'I told you so' in your head right now."

"I'm not one to gloat," Plato said. "But it's good that you have a backup option since you can't use magic here."

Bouncing the beam of light around the tunnel, Liv searched, unsure what she was looking for. A round blue and green stone in the center of the space caught her eye. She strode over, recognizing how similar it was to the circle on which she stood in the Chamber of the Tree. Symbols like those in the House of Seven were etched around the circle.

"Can you read it?" Plato asked.

She squinted at the symbols, hoping that would help. "No. Why, *should* I be able to?"

"You have the ability as a Warrior of the House, but the skill hadn't developed yet."

Liv knelt, rubbing her hands over the symbols. As she

had guessed they would, they danced and glowed under her fingers, responding to her touch.

Something pinched her in the leg and Liv stood suddenly, pushing her hand into the pocket of her pants to find out what was poking her. She withdrew her mother's ring.

The symbols on the ground began to shift, rearranging themselves. Liv put the ring in the palm of her hand and the symbols froze, looking as they had before.

She glanced at Plato. "Are you seeing what I'm seeing?"

"No, I don't believe I am," he stated. "What do you see?"

She opened her fingers and picked up the ring, sliding it over the symbols. They floated into the air, transforming into a language she understood. "The ring decodes the ancient language."

Plato took a step forward. "And now you know one of its purposes, although there must be more."

"Like the wall in the library," Liv said.

"What do the symbols say?"

Liv pulled the ring away and the symbols reappeared. Again she ran the ring over the symbols, and again they morphed. It says, "Look toward the heavens. Climb high to reach the treasure."

Liv's chin tilted backward and she looked up, realizing at once that she was under one of the towers of the castle, which rose probably ten stories. Around the wall of the round room were pushed out rocks that formed small ledges. They went around and around, all the way up to the top.

"You've got to be kidding me," Liv said dryly. "There has to be another way."

"You can't use magic, so I don't think there is," Plato said.

She growled at him. "You're the cat who always lands on his feet. Why don't *you* climb up there and let me know what's in the room?"

"We both know I don't need to climb to get up there, but I also can't go up there without you."

"How's that?" Liv asked.

"I just tried. Something's preventing it. I'm guessing I need a House member to invite me."

"How come I can't use magic here, but you can do your Houdini act?"

"My magic doesn't have the same restrictions as yours," Plato explained.

"You're a very strange creature." Liv slid her mother's ring onto her finger and put her flashlight in her mouth since she'd need both hands to climb. She pulled herself up onto the first ledge, which was about three feet off the ground. It was so narrow that half of her foot hung over the side. Each block was roughly two feet long and the distance to the next ledge was about the same, but each was a foot or so higher. It was like a really shitty staircase.

It was evident to Liv that she was going to need her hands to climb and her mouth was getting tired already, so she put the flashlight in her pocket with the beam of light facing up so she could still see.

Carefully, Liv jumped to the next ledge, gripping the wall for balance. The rough stones gave her some purchase, but she recognized that wouldn't save her if she lost her balance.

The higher Liv climbed, the less inclined she was to

jump from step to step. There was no magic to save her if she fell. There was no one to save her either, not that she regretted telling Stefan to buzz off. Liv wasn't a princess in a tower looking for a hero. She was a Warrior, climbing to the top of a tower in a castle for justice's sake.

Plato appeared a few steps up, looking down at her as she continued the trek. As she got close to the slab he was on, he disappeared and reappeared a few ledges up.

"Are you trying to tease me with how easy this is for you?" Liv said, sweating.

"I'm supervising," he said simply.

Liv's foot slipped as she stepped onto the next ledge, and her knee banged into the stone. Her hands caught the rock at the last moment as her legs dangled under her. She tried to pull herself up, but couldn't manage it. Instead, she swung her legs to the side, catching the step she'd just come off with her foot. Once she was sure she had it, she pushed off the stone she was holding, bracing herself against the wall.

For a long minute, Liv breathed hard, pressing her cheek to the stone. When her heart had slowed down, she opened her eyes to find Plato regarding her calmly from up high.

"I need to work out more," she told him.

"I thought you handled that near-fall well."

"I couldn't do a pull-up, which is going to change when I get out of here."

"I can't do a pull-up either if it makes you feel better."

"It doesn't." Liv stepped carefully to the next ledge, keeping her center low. She continued to move like that around the tower, getting into a rhythm as she climbed higher and higher.

She didn't mean to, but when she was close to the top, Liv looked down. She immediately regretted it. "Holy shit! It's a long way to the bottom."

"So don't fall," Plato said, now a step below her.

"Thanks. Your advice is stellar, as always."

"Anytime," Plato replied.

There were only five more steps to the top, which led to an opening in the ceiling of the tower. Liv had no idea what she was climbing up to and risking her life for, but everything she had found had led her there. Whatever was at the top of this tower, she'd face it.

She looked back at Plato when there was only one more step left. "Can you still not get into the room?"

He shook his head. "You have to go first. I need you to invite me in."

Liv swallowed, turning back to the ledge. She ducked her head so as to avoid hitting the ceiling and crawled onto the last step, poking her head through the hole. Then something she hadn't expected during the long, arduous climb happened. The ledge she was standing on shifted, partially falling out of the wall. Liv grabbed the edge of the hole, her feet kicking. The stone dislodged from the wall completely, tumbling to the ground below.

Liv nearly screamed as her legs dangled. She tried to find the step before the last one, but it was too far away. Liv tried to find her footing on the wall, but her hands kept slipping. She was blind, looking at the stone in front of her, and her fingers had cramped. She was sure she was about to fall to her death when her boot found the hole the stone had fallen out of. Liv sucked in a breath as she regained her balance; her heart felt ready to jump out of her chest. Although she had saved herself, Liv didn't want to stay there much longer.

"I'm freaking getting strong enough to do a pull-up," she said, emphasizing each word as she pushed off with her feet and pulled herself up through the hole.

When she'd cleared it, Liv pushed away, trying to put some distance between the hole and her.

Blinking to clear her vision, Liv realized that this room was much brighter than the tower she'd just come from. She stood, her breath hitching in her throat. Liv didn't know what she had expected to find in this room, but what she saw was definitely not it.

CHAPTER THIRTY-THREE

L iv had come all this way and nearly fallen to her death to try to determine what had happened to one canister of stolen magic. She spun around, her mouth hanging open as she gaped at the hundreds of canisters lining the shelves that filled the circular room. Glowing blue canisters sat on top of one another on dusty shelves.

"What in the world?" Liv whispered.

"Well, now we know what happened to the canister," Plato said, now beside her. "It joined the others."

"Who is hoarding all this magic? And why?" Liv stepped closer to the first row, reaching out to touch a canister. It glowed brighter when her finger grazed the glass.

"And storing it in a monastery run by mortals." Plato strolled around the room, inspecting the contents.

"I fear we have more questions than we do answers at this point."

Liv followed his path, lost in a daze as she walked around the small room. "I just don't understand why this is here, or how it got all the way up here. Climbing up was terrifying. I couldn't imagine doing that with a canister of magic as many times as it would have taken to get all these up here."

Plato stopped in front of the hole in the wall, peering down at the floor far below. "May not be a good time to bring this up, but have you figured out how you're getting down with that first step broken?"

Liv pressed her eyes closed, feeling stuck. "Yeah, I don't know. I guess I'll be living here. Maybe you can go back and tell Clark to come and rescue me, although I'm not sure how he'll do it without using magic."

"Isn't it ironic that you can't do magic in the monastery, and that's where all this magic is being stored?" Plato asked.

Liv scratched her head, tension making it ache. "I don't understand anything that is happening here."

A soft hissing at Liv's back made her straighten. "Please tell me that was you, Plato."

"It wasn't."

Liv tentatively turned around not seeing anything at first, only the glow of the canisters. Then she saw them—two bright yellow eyes staring at her from behind two canisters. Were there rats up here? she wondered, stepping back.

The eyes moved forward, and a snake's head materialized between the canisters. Gracefully, the snake slithered down from the lowest shelf, its body winding around the canisters. It had to be over twelve feet long.

"Ummm, Plato? What do you make of this?"

"It's a lophos," Plato said, and for the first time in their five years together, there was an edge of fear to his voice.

"A lophos?" Liv asked as he took the position beside her.

"It is a magical serpent that doesn't age or need food to survive. It's used to guard important items, and when someone trespasses into its territory, it paralyzes them using hypnotism."

"How do I fight it?" Liv asked.

"That's the thing. You can't."

"Can't? Do you mean I can't without magic?"

Slithering to the ground, the serpent moved back and forth like a silky ribbon.

"Liv, there is no spell that will stop a lophos' hypnotism."

The snake hissed, a long melodic sound that laced around Liv's thoughts, carrying her off to a faraway place.

"But you'll be okay? Can you get out of here? Go back and get Clark."

Plato swayed, his head lolling. "Liv," he said his words slurring. "Lynxes have many enemies, but none more dangerous to us than the lophos. I can't combat..."

The cat slumped to the stone floor.

"Oh no, you didn't," Liv found herself saying, although she didn't know why. It was hard for her to remember exactly where she was. All she knew was, some dumbass snake had just messed with her cat.

The snake hissed again, its long forked tongue flicking out of its mouth.

Liv shook her head, trying to dispel the strange feelings

attempting to take over her. She bent over, scooping Plato's limp body from the floor and cradling him to her chest. "Look, I get that you have a job to protect this magic. I'm not here to take it. I'm trying to figure out…" Liv's voice trailed off as she tried to remember why she was holding a strange cat and standing in a room with a bunch of glowing snow globes.

Wait, they weren't snow globes. They were magic, and she was a magician. This was Plato. And there was still one more chance to save them.

Her mind wasn't gone yet, but it would be soon, and then they'd die there.

But that wasn't going to happen. This was not Liv Beaufont's last day on Earth. Not even close. She reached out and grabbed the closest canister of magic.

The snake lunged at her, its hiss growing in intensity.

Liv jerked the lid off the canister as the snake shot forward. It struck, biting her in the leg and making her double over with a pain she had never conceived of. Its venom filled her veins, and she thought she'd die there from the bite rather than waste away in a hypnotic state. However, the canister was open.

Liv forced herself to dip her hand into it. She lifted it into the air and blew, hoping against hope that it formed a portal. The reasoning was that personal magic couldn't be used in the monastery, as if it was somehow locked. But a third-party source of magic could be used—like the canisters.

The portal shone in the room, the best thing Liv had ever seen. She didn't step through it like she intended but instead fell into the entrance to another place, carrying Plato and the canister with her, hoping the lophos didn't follow. She didn't want that magical monster taking over her thoughts for the rest of her life—if she had much more life to live, which she prayed she did.

CHAPTER THIRTY-FOUR

L iv's head hit the side table next to her couch when she fell out of the portal, into her apartment. With no time to worry about her newest injury, she closed the portal immediately, not wanting the lophos to follow her.

She released Plato, who was still passed out, and cradled her leg. Blood was everywhere, soaking onto her carpet.

Her head swam as she looked around the apartment, trying to figure out what to do next. She needed help but felt close to passing out from the snake's venom. It burned in her veins, making her leg feel like it was on fire.

With a shaking hand, Liv pulled out her cell phone. Barely strong enough to hold the phone to her head, she switched it to speaker and rolled over on her side, her face mushed into the carpet.

The phone rang once.

Twice.

Liv's eyes fluttered shut. Staying conscious felt impossible.

Again the phone rang.

"Hello? What happened?" Clark asked in a rush.

"I need help—" Liv wanted to say more, but couldn't. The venom sent her into a blackness that felt never-ending.

"It would be a lot easier to know what bit her if she was conscious to tell us," a woman's voice said, stirring Liv from the haze holding her hostage.

Impatient footsteps echoed on the floor one way and then the other. "How does it look?" Clark asked, his voice tense.

"I've extracted the venom," the woman replied. "But without knowing what kind of snake it was, I can't treat her properly."

"L-L-L," Liv muttered, still locked away.

"Liv." Clark rushed over, grabbing her hand. "You're awake."

Not really, she thought, trying to break free of whatever was keeping her in the strange blackness. She sensed the light on the other side of her eyelids, but no matter how hard she tried, she couldn't open her eyes—something she realized she'd taken for granted all her life.

"Why doesn't she wake up?" Clark asked, pushing her hair back from her face.

"I'm not sure," the woman said. "What do you think she's trying to say?"

"L-Lo-Lo," Liv stuttered, unsure if she was actually speaking out loud or just in her head.

Clark leaned down, putting his ear close to her mouth. "What are you saying? Lo-what?"

"Lophos," Plato said, his voice groggy but clear enough.

A gasp fell out of the woman's mouth. "A *lophos* bit her? Where... Never mind that. I know exactly what I have to do now."

"What's a lophos?" Clark asked. "Will she be all right?"

"I need to work now," the woman answered. "And she's not going to wake up until I heal her of that bite. The poison will keep her asleep."

Liv reached out, finding Clark's hand again. She squeezed it with as much force as she could muster, not knowing if it was enough for him to register. He gripped her back and rubbed his thumb over the back of her hand. "I know you're in there. Hold on and we'll fix you. I promise."

"I told him that she had a bug," Clark said from the other side of the room, his voice exhausted. "And then what? He told you?"

"She's been out for almost two days," Rory's familiar voice said. "I knew something was up. And John will think something's up too if we're not careful."

"I just don't understand," Clark stated. "When is she going to wake up?"

"The lophos' bite is lethal," Rory replied. "The fact that she's still alive is incredible."

"I know you're trying to make me feel better, but it's not working."

"I would never dream of making you feel better, magician," Rory said.

Liv called out in her mind, screaming that she was awake, and yet she knew they heard nothing. She was trapped. Trapped on the other side of a blurry wall where she could hear everything but no one could hear her.

The recurring dream was always the same. The pack of wolves chased Liv, gaining on her. Safety was just up ahead. A house. Unlocked. All she had to do was get there. Throw the door shut behind her. This time the wolves wouldn't catch her before she got to the house.

Every time the dream ended the same way. First the claws, then the teeth. The wolves always carried her away screaming, pain radiating from where their teeth bit into her leg. Always the same place. And then the dream ended, only to start up again later.

But this time, she was running faster. Getting ahead of them. This time, she wouldn't lose.

The house was close. So close. She ran onto the porch, leaping over the steps.

Her hand was on the door handle when she looked back. The wolves had halted a few yards away, their teeth bared and their eyes narrowed.

Liv swung the door open and nearly bolted forward. However, she stopped herself. It wasn't a house at all, but rather a bluff leading to a dangerous fall that ended in a rocky ocean.

Liv turned back to the wolves, and then, without hesitation, she jumped off the cliff, plummeting to what she feared was her death.

Shooting to a sitting position, Liv sucked in a loud gasp, her voice aching to be released. She clapped her hands to her chest, pressing against her heart, which had never beat so fast.

Clark's head whipped up. He was sitting on the other side of the room, but rushed over at once, his eyes wide with shock. "You're awake!"

There were a thousand things Liv wanted to say, and yet she had no voice. Every time she opened her mouth to speak, only ragged breath fell out.

"Here, drink this," Clark said. "We've been trying to keep your reserves up as best we could with magic, but nothing replaces eating and drinking the old-fashioned way."

Liv's hands were shaking when she took the glass, nearly banging it into her teeth as she drank. She drained the entire glass, feeling like the cracks in her throat were mending already. "How...how...how long?"

Clark nodded, seeming to understand her question at once. His usually perfectly slicked back blond hair was a mess, falling over his forehead. His clothes were wrinkled, the sleeves of his button-up rolled to the elbow and covered in spots of blood. "Three days. It's been three days since you called me."

Liv looked around her tiny apartment, noticing potion bottles and other items that didn't belong to her. Plato was curled up next to her leg, the one where she'd been bitten.

She managed to smile at the cat, whose eyes glistened back at her in quiet appreciation. On the table next to them was the canister of magic, the one that had saved her.

Liv swung her legs to the side, wanting to stand, but realizing at once that her body was too stiff to move quickly.

"Hey, take it easy," Clark warned. "I'll call Hester to have a look at you."

"Hester?" Liv asked.

A dark shadow fell across Clark's face. "I didn't have a choice. When I found you, I didn't know who else to call. She's the best healer the House has."

"But she's a Councilor," Liv argued, her stomach aching with hunger all of a sudden.

Clark stood, pulling his phone from his pocket. "I think she can be trusted. Anyway, I didn't give her any information, and she didn't ask. She just worked to fix you, and it appears that against the odds, she succeeded." He held the phone to his ear, walking toward the door. "It won't take her long to get here, but don't try to get up. I'll be right back."

Clark whispered into the phone as he paced to the door.

Liv looked down at Plato, letting out a weighty sigh. "So we survived."

He pressed his head into her arm, affectionately rubbing the side of his face against her fingers as she petted him. "Because of your quick thinking. Thank you for saving me."

Liv smiled easily. "I was just returning the favor. You've saved me loads of times."

Clark returned a moment later, looking Liv over like he

thought she might have changed in the minute since he'd left her. "She'll be here soon. How do you feel?"

"Like I've been asleep for three days and need a steak dinner," Liv answered.

Clark laughed, and it seemed to melt away some of the stress around his eyes. "Yeah, I second that. A steak would be perfect right now."

"Have you been here ever since you found me?" Liv asked.

He nodded, looking down at his messy clothes.

"What does the House think?"

"Don't worry," Clark said, waving off her concern. "I told them I had other business, and they think you're away working on your case. I never take a day off, so it wasn't disputed."

"Yeah, but that's just the thing," Liv argued. "You never take a day off. Don't you think that will draw suspicion?"

Clark lowered his chin, exhaustion evident in his movements. "Liv, I thought you were going to die. I didn't really care what the House thought." When he looked at her, the pain he was usually so good at hiding was written plainly on his face.

"I'm sorry. You must have been worried. If something happened to me, the Beaufonts would lose their place—"

Clark shook his head, new conviction in his eyes. "No, you don't get it. This has never been about us keeping our place in the House, Liv. This is about us. We've lost so much. Mom and Dad. Ian and Reese. I can't lose you. The House is second in my priorities. Family is what matters now."

Tears ached in Liv's dry throat, begging to be released.

She managed a smile as a single tear rolled down her cheek. "*Familia est sempiternum*."

Clark's eyes fell to the canister. He pointed, obviously trying to break the tension. "You got back the stolen canister of magic. That's something."

Liv couldn't stop herself from laughing, which made her think she might pass out. She lifted the glass in Clark's direction, silently asking for more.

"Actually, I brought back that one by mistake. Recovering all of the canisters would take several trips," Liv said, telling Clark the whole story as he refilled her glass with water.

"I don't understand," Clark said, taking a seat in the chair next to her. "What are they doing there? Why would someone store magic like that and use a lophos to protect it?"

Liv drained the glass, feeling her strength returning. "I don't know, but we definitely have more investigating to do. When I'm back to normal, I've got to check out the wall with the symbols in the library."

Clark agreed with a nod. "Yes, the ring. It sounds like it will explain a lot."

"I plan to learn the ancient language. I believe it holds the key to this mystery." They both looked up, having the same epiphany.

"Key," Clark said in a hushed voice.

"Do you think that was what Reese was referring to when she said, 'Olivia has the key?'" Liv asked.

Clark nodded, running his hands over his stubbly cheeks. "Yes, and you said Ian left the ring for you. If you're right and it opens something in the library, well, we need to check it out."

Liv tried to stand again but was met with defeat, her legs too weak to support her. Clark darted forward, catching her and helping her back down.

"But for now, you need to rest. The ring and the wall can wait," he told her sternly. "You need to recover."

Reluctantly, Liv agreed, pushing back on the sofa. "Yes, and we don't know what the other part of Reese's message means, about you having the heart."

"I'll figure it—"

The front door opening cut off Clark's words.

Hester was a strange sight as she strode into Liv's apartment, her traveling cloak partially covering her spikey gray hair. She smiled sincerely at Liv when she laid her eyes on her. "Well, I haven't seen such a wonderful sight in a long time. It is nice to see you awake."

Liv looked down at her bandaged leg. "Thank you for healing me. I can explain—"

Hester hurried over, gesturing for Liv to put her leg back up. "Let me have a look, and then maybe you can explain. Or maybe you shouldn't." She tilted her chin down, looking at Liv over her half-moon spectacles. "I mean, the Council doesn't need to know everything. A girl is entitled to have a private life."

Liv smiled, putting her legs back on the sofa.

"And I might have healed the surface wounds, but if you awoke from the lophos bite, it was due to sheer determination on your part," Hester continued, unbandaging her leg. "Sometimes the most amazing things in life have nothing to do with magic."

Liv wasn't ready for the disgusting sight of her leg

when the bandages were removed. Two large black puncture wounds covered the side of her calf, red spider-like veins fanning out from them.

"Well, this looks much better," Hester said, a smile springing to her face.

"This looks better?" Liv asked with a laugh, grimacing at her leg.

"You should have seen it to begin with," Clark said, looking over Hester's shoulder at the wound. "Your leg was covered in blood. I didn't even know it was a bite until I called Hester."

Nausea hit Liv's stomach. She remembered falling through the portal and looking down at her leg and thinking it was the end. It appeared that she had been given another chance. A chance to solve the mystery of the House of Seven and bring the justice her parents fought for, and to be a part of the family she didn't think she wanted for so long.

The tender knot has risen in Liv's throat again, making her fear more tears would spill from her eyes. "Will the scar fade?" Liv asked Hester in an attempt to cover her emotion.

The healer ran her hand over Liv's leg, her fingers vibrating but not touching. She opened her hazel eyes and gave Liv a thoughtful look. "I can't say. Bites have their own way of healing, and it is usually unique to the person it happens to. But I do think you'll make a full recovery."

"That's great," Liv said, taking a deep breath and feeling some of the weight evaporating.

"I'm truly happy to tell you that," Hester said. "Bites

aren't my specialty. Between you and Stefan, my healing abilities have really been challenged lately."

"Stefan?" Liv asked, surprised to hear the name. "He was bitten? By a snake?"

Hester's expression gave away her mistake. "Oh, no. And it was nothing. I shouldn't have said anything. My apologies. Spending this time here with you and your brother away from the House of Seven has brought down my walls." The healer stood, giving Liv a sudden serious look. "But at the House, we should remember our places and act as prescribed. I think that is for the best. Don't you?"

Clark stepped forward, nodding. "I agree. And I'm hoping that you won't make the same slip about Liv and me in anyone else's company?"

Hester thought for a moment. "Yes, I think it would be best if we all forgot about this. I'm not sure what you were up to when you were bitten, Liv, but I urge you to be careful in the future. Things in the House are shifting, and I daresay you might be the cause of it. Whatever the case, I trust the Beaufont family. I can't say that about many in the House."

Relief filled Clark's face. "We trust you, and Trudy too. Thank you for your discretion."

Hester's gaze drifted to the canister of magic sitting on the table. "I believe we have a rough road ahead of us at the House. There are those who are good, those who are bad, and those who are in a gray zone. That's how life works, though. Many of us at the House are afraid of what will come if we fight back and afraid what will happen if we don't. I'm not happy to say that's created cowards of many of us, and yet, I believe our hearts are in the right place. What we need is someone to reset the balance. That was the goal of the House of Seven all along, wasn't it?"

"Yes," Liv said, her pulse echoing the excitement building in her chest. "That's what we're—"

Hester held up her hand, cutting Liv off. "I believe the less I know, the better. I am a Councilor, after all, and our job is to be objective. Yours as a Warrior is to have courage, and I think you've exemplified that through all." She looked around as if she might be forgetting something, then nodded in the direction of the door. "Yes, I think I'll be taking my leave now. Goodbye, Liv." Offering Clark a polite nod, she said, "I'll be seeing you later, Clark."

He escorted her to the door and returned a moment later with a small package wrapped in brown paper.

"What's that?" Liv asked.

"It was on the doorstep. I just found it," he said, hesitating when he was about to hand it to her.

"That's Rory's writing," Liv stated, reading the inscription on the front.

To: Liv Beaufont

From: Rory Laurens

"Oh," Clark replied, relinquishing the package to Liv. "I messaged him right after calling Hester to let him know you'd awoken. He was worried." Clark grimaced a bit on the last sentence.

"That's right, you met the giant," she said with a laugh, untying the string holding the package together.

Clark gave her a look of surprise. "How do you know that?"

"When I was asleep, I was, well, sort of not," Liv

explained. "I could hear certain things. I was trapped in sleep, though, and unable to respond when I heard you talking and worrying."

Liv stopped opening the package and looked up at her big brother. "So you made nice with the giant, did you?"

He sort of shrugged. "I could see he was worried about you. He came by when I'd sent word to John that you were too sick to make your shift, and he wouldn't take 'sod off' for an answer."

Liv laughed. "No, Rory is a bit of a mother goose, but don't tell him I said that. Actually, you should. It will make that wrinkle between his eyebrows deeper."

"Eyebrows plural?" Clark asked. "I only counted the one."

Liv reached out to slap her brother's arm, but he was fast enough to pull away in time. That wouldn't last for much longer though. Not once her strength was back.

"Be nice. Rory is a good guy."

"What did he send?" Clark pointed to the package.

Liv looked down at the package, but another question occurred to her. "John? Is he okay? Does he suspect anything?"

Clark gave her an uncertain look. "I'm not sure. I told him you were sick, but something tells me he won't feel better until he sets his eyes on you."

Liv nodded. "Yeah, I'm sure it's been hard for him. And he's been covering my shift. I should get down there—"

Clark shook his head, cutting her off again. "Rest. That's what you're going to do, and I'm going to tell John that you're recovering. I'll tell him to come up and see you when I leave, but keep that wound covered. We don't need anyone asking questions."

Liv agreed, continuing to open the package Rory had sent. The smell of cinnamon and cloves hit her as she unwrapped a loaf of spice bread. On top of it was a note, also in Rory's handwriting:

When you're better, come by. I have something that belongs to you.

Liv smiled, unwrapping the bread and breaking off a piece for Clark, offering it to him.

"The giant sent you bread?" he asked, eyeing the piece skeptically.

"Take it," Liv implored. "You look like you haven't eaten this whole time either. And yes, the giant is a great baker. Turning this down is a bad idea."

Clark resigned his hesitation and took the bread, popping it in his mouth. His face transformed with surprise. "Hey, that's pretty good."

"Yeah, see? You *can* make things without magic," Liv said, taking a bite and enjoying the rich flavors that exploded in her mouth.

"You know what? For the first time in a long time, I'm starting to see that you're right. What Hester said was true. The best things in life have nothing to do with magic."

Liv smiled, staring at her brother with a fondness she hadn't felt in a long, long time. "Magic is a bonus. It should always be a bonus in an already wonderful and full life."

CHAPTER THIRTY-FIVE

W alking was more difficult than Liv would have liked. She'd missed work for two more days, trying to regain her strength. The guilt kept her up after John messaged her, asking how she was doing. Clark had told him that she had an awful flu and it was better to stay away.

"What am I going to say when he asks why I'm limping?" Liv asked, pulling her pants over her bandage, careful to not open the wound back up. She still couldn't look at it without feeling sick.

"Maybe he won't notice," Plato reasoned, watching from his perch on the side of the sofa.

Liv laughed, half-dragging her leg behind her as she trudged to the kitchen. "I think he's going to notice."

"Tell him that you were delirious while you had the flu and slipped and fell in your bathtub. You were going to call him for help, but you were naked and embarrassed," Plato offered. "After an excuse like that, he won't ask another question, especially if you add some details like that you pulled down the shower curtain in the process and have a nasty bruise on your a—"

"That's enough," Liv said, cutting the cat off. "And I'm done with telling him lies. It's wrong. I may not know how to tell him the truth, but I don't have to fill him full of lies."

"Okay, then tell him you were bitten by a magical snake while trapped at the top of a monastery during a search for stolen magic. I think that will go over much better."

"Good idea. But I'll leave out the monastery part," Liv said seriously. "John can't stand churches, so that might derail the story."

Plato laughed, something he didn't do very often but had been doing more since they returned from the monastery. He also hadn't left the apartment, which was unlike him. Usually he disappeared at least once every day, not giving any explanation for his absence and sometimes smelling of smoke or strange herbs.

Although the commute to work was only a few blocks, Liv knew that her leg couldn't handle the exercise. Therefore, she created a portal to John's shop, careful to place it in the back alley. She stepped through the shimmering blue and green archway, grateful that her magic had returned after she refilled her reserves.

She and Plato exited the portal, nearly walking into John as he carried a box to the dumpster. He jumped back, startled by her sudden presence. He dropped the box, a broken keyboard and other parts falling out.

"Oh, jeez, you scared me," John said, grabbing his chest.

"I'm sorry," Liv said, turning around to ensure that the portal had disappeared. "I didn't mean to. Are you okay?"

John took several breaths to regain his composure. Liv

worried that the scare had overly taxed his heart, but he broke into sudden laughter, cutting through her tension. "Where did you come from? It's like you appeared out of nowhere."

Liv again looked back at where the portal had been. Mortals usually didn't see a magician coming through a portal. If they did, it was explained logically in their mind somehow. The fact that it seemed to John as if she'd just appeared resolved a question she'd been debating during the last few days. For whatever reason, the veil between John and the magical world had come down. Maybe it was because Liv and Rory were around him so often, or maybe because he was an open-minded individual. Each person was different, Clark had explained during one of the long conversations they'd had the last few days.

He'd told her that many times telling a mortal the truth about magic simply didn't work. They couldn't see the magic because it didn't work in their construct. That was why most of them didn't see portals or many other magical things that happened around them. However, as mortals were exposed more and more to magic, they saw the things that they had ignored before.

Clark still thought that telling a mortal about magic was dangerous because it put them in a magician's world. However, Liv had debated this long enough, and keeping John in the dark was putting him in worse danger. He didn't even know there was anything to be on his guard about. John had served in the military; he was one of the strongest people she knew. Knowing what was out there and that there was a potential danger was better than being ignorant. At least, that was what Liv wanted to believe.

"John we need to talk," Liv said, gesturing toward the open back door.

"Is everything okay? Are you feeling better? You don't have to be at work if you're still ill."

"Are you kidding? If I have to stare at the walls in my apartment for another minute, I'm going to scream."

John chuckled, waving her forward. "Okay, well, you go ahead, then."

Liv did as she was told and counted the seconds until his next words.

"Are you limping?"

"Yeah, I sort of hurt myself," Liv said, taking longer than she'd like to travel to the main workstation in the back. She took a seat on the stool and motioned to the other one. "You should sit down for this. I have something I have to tell you."

John hesitated, raising a bushy eyebrow at her. "Are you quitting? Is this about that other job of yours?"

"No and yes," Liv replied. "Go on, though. Sit down."

John did as he was told as Plato jumped up on the workstation, taking a front-row seat for the show.

Liv cleared her throat. She didn't know how to tell John the next part. She'd known about magic all her life and felt it coursing through her veins. She couldn't even conceive of a reality magic wasn't a part of, so how did she explain it to someone who didn't have the same perspective as her? How did she explain this so that John still liked her and didn't think she was a crazy person?

"I know I've been different lately, and you've witnessed new things happening in my life," Liv began. "There's a perfectly good explanation for it all, but you're going to have to give me a chance to explain it fully, which might take some time."

"You're a magician," John said with a smile on his face.

Liv's mouth popped open. She waited for him to laugh. To tell her he was joking and ready to hear what she had to say.

John scooted off his stool and disappeared into his office. When he returned, he was carrying a photo album she'd never seen. He must have read the surprise on her face because he held it up and said, "I keep this hidden under a loose floorboard. You're not the only one who has secrets, but as long as you're being honest, I should be too."

Liv was speechless. She looked between Plato and John, wondering if they were pulling a joke on her.

Setting the album in front of Liv, John opened it to the first page. A musty scent like an attic had been opened after a long time wafted up from the book. On the first page was a picture of John standing next to a woman wearing a white gown. She was beautiful, with long flowing brown hair and a crown of flowers. Beside her, John wore a loose suit, and on his face was the largest grin she'd ever seen him wear.

"This is my wife, Chloe," John said, smiling fondly at the picture.

"Wait, you have a wife? How did I not know that?"

John looked at her thoughtfully. "For the same reason that you're just now confiding in me that you're a magician. And Chloe *was* my wife. She's been gone for many, many years."

"How did you know I was a magician?" Liv had so many

questions that she didn't even know where to begin. She'd rehearsed this speech, and it hadn't gone this way at all.

"I didn't, at first. Maybe I had hints of it over the years, but I never thought much about it," John explained. "You see, Chloe and I were high school sweethearts. I asked for her hand in marriage after we graduated, and she turned me down. She ran across the country but I followed her, knowing that couldn't be the end of us. It took me a long time to track her down." He chuckled, his eyes distant as if he saw the memory in his mind. "You should have seen her face when I walked into the café where she was waiting tables. Much like you, Chloe liked working with her hands. She liked a good, honest day of work."

"Wait, she turned down your proposal and you stalked her? John, that's super-creepy."

He nodded, laughing. "I realize that now, but I was in love, and I didn't believe her when she said she didn't want to marry me. There was something missing, and I didn't want to live, not knowing what that was."

"Chloe was a magician," Liv guessed.

"That's right," John said, looking down at the photo before them. "She didn't think I'd understand how different her life was. Man, I thought she was exaggerating, but I later learned that she hadn't been. I begged her to allow me into her life. I told her I'd do anything to make it work."

"And she accepted," Liv stated.

"Well, not at first. She was reluctant, saying that it was dangerous for mortals to live in a magician's world," John said, his expression dark. "But I didn't give up. I showed up every day at that café, demonstrating to her however she'd let me that I was serious about us being together."

"Again, you sound like a stalker," Liv told him with a laugh. "And you didn't find it strange when she said she was a magician? You didn't think she was making it up?"

"I'll admit, at first I thought it was a wild excuse, but Chloe had never lied to me, so I knew it was the truth. She'd been secretive, sure, but she'd always been honest with me, and I could feel that."

Liv had often felt that John was incredibly intuitive, knowing things she was going to do before she did them. It wasn't hard for her to believe he'd had this sort of insight into Chloe.

"And to answer your question, I didn't know what to think about this magician business," John continued. "At first I couldn't retain the things Chloe shared with me. I'd simply forget seeing her using her magic. Later she'd mention it, and I'd have no memory. However, over time, magic became a part of my life, too. Her life was weird and I didn't know what to make of it at first, but I had her, and that was what I wanted most."

"So you two got married," Liv said, flipping through the album, looking at a John who was easily thirty years younger. He laughed a lot in the photos, his eyes always on Chloe.

"Yes, and when I went away to serve, I knew that our love was strong enough to survive the time apart." John's expression turned dark again. All the joy he'd shown moments prior disappeared from his eyes. "However, when I returned, ready to really start our life together, Chloe was different. She was distant, when before she'd allowed me into her life. She was always looking over her shoulder, waking up in the middle of the night. One day she left a note that said I didn't work in her life anymore, and there was nothing that could change that." He shook his head, his chin low. "The letter said all the things you'd expect. She said it wasn't me, it was her. She stated that we were too different and that she worried about our future, so therefore there couldn't be one for us. Then she asked that I let her go and not search for her."

Pickles lifted his paws onto John's leg as if sensing he needed the extra comfort. John reached down and picked up the dog, staring into his dark brown eyes for a long moment. "That was almost four decades ago."

"So you didn't go after her?"

"No. She'd asked me not to," John said.

"But you didn't listen to her the first time when she turned down your proposal."

"I knew she was hiding something, and that she still wanted me. However, the tone in Chloe's letter was different than before. My wife was different. Before, she'd been warm and full of joy, but when I returned, something in her had died. She wasn't the woman I had married. I tried to understand, but the more I tried, the harder she pushed me away. So when she asked me to let her go, I knew that was what I had to do. And I suppose that in a way, she was right. Mortals and magicians aren't meant to be. I know Chloe worried what would happen if we had a family."

Liv's heart ached. She could hardly believe that the man she'd known for the past five years had such a story to tell. She hadn't even had a chance to assimilate the implications of what John had just shared. "So you knew I was a magician?"

"I only started to piece things together recently, although I think I was in denial at the same time." John scratched Pickles' head. "You know I think of you as a daughter. When I started to feel the magic around you the way I had felt it with Chloe, I worried that it would take you away. And you've gotten more distant, and been off on secret adventures. Then you had magicians and fae showing up here, and I just assumed that soon you'd leave me too."

"What? You knew that Clark and Rudolf were magical? Were you never going to say anything to me about this if I hadn't admitted it to you today?" Liv asked.

John shrugged. "Of course. It's sort of obvious just looking at them. And, I'm a firm believer in allowing the people in my life to have their privacy, and I know that it isn't easy for magicians to explain this to mortals."

Liv looked at Plato, shaking her head before directing her gaze back to John. "This is so strange. Here I thought I was going to have to convince you that I wasn't making this all up. Now I find out that you were married to a magician."

John slapped his knee, a pleased expression breaking through the tension on his face. "Okay, so start at the beginning. Tell me everything you can."

"Well, I'm not sure... I only had my magic unlocked recently."

John nodded, giving her a sideways grin. "Yes, that was when all the strange things started to happen. My calculator added up numbers before I typed them in."

"Yeah, sorry about that. I've been trying to avoid my magic having unintended consequences. If you don't want me using magic at work, I completely understand."

John scoffed. "Are you kidding? Since you've gotten your magic, the shop has never run so smoothly. It's clean as can be, and our turnaround time on repairs is keeping customers happy." He leaned forward, holding Pickles to his chest and giving Liv a conspiratorial look. "Actually, now that we're being honest, I feel like I might be taking advantage of your talents, benefitting as a business owner. I'm hoping I'm not putting you in an awkward position."

"Not at all," Liv said at once. "No, it's me who feels like I'm putting you in danger. That's why I'm telling you the truth now. I feel like you should have a choice and know the facts. I'm a magician. Specifically, I'm a Warrior of the House of Seven, and I make enemies patrolling the magical world. Strange things happen around me. Strange people visit me. The line between my old life and my new one is blurred, and I need you to know that and tell me if it isn't okay with you. Because the last thing I want to do is put you and your business in danger."

John considered her words for a long time, his eyes searching the ground without really seeing it. "I've heard of the House of Seven before. Chloe didn't always have nice things to say about it."

Liv nodded. "That's not uncommon. Some magicians don't like the regulations the House puts on the community, but its overarching goal of justice is a good one."

"And you work for them now?" John asked. "That's the other job you have?"

"Yes, but it's at night, and I can handle doing both."

When she released him, she was arrested by the tender look on his face. It made him look so much younger, as if their moment of honesty and emotion had magically transformed him. "John, I'm not going anywhere. I want to believe that the two races can exist together, not separately like they have for so long. Don't ever worry that I'm going anywhere. As long as you're okay with a freak magician and her talking cat, I'm sticking around."

John looked at Plato suddenly. "The cat can talk?"

"Oh, yeah," Liv said. "Go ahead, show him, Plato."

The lynx yawned and settled down on his stomach, resting his head on his paws.

John looked at her sideways. "You're sure you're a magician and not just certifiably insane?"

"I'm both," Liv said.

John pushed up from the stool, setting Pickles on the floor. "Well, now that this business is out of the way, I have an important question for you."

Liv looked up at him curiously.

"Where's that carrot cake you promised to bring me? I'm starving."

CHAPTER THIRTY-SIX

Rory's front door was open when Liv arrived at his house that afternoon. Plato halted on the threshold, sniffing the air.

"Oh, come on," she said, waving him in. "They are only kittens."

"They are annoying little beasts," Plato countered.

"Well, lookie there. You *can* talk," Liv stated, narrowing her eyes at the cat. "Maybe next time you won't make me look like a fool. John still doesn't buy that you can talk. He believes that I can fix things with magic and faced off an evil serpent, but he drew the line at a talking cat."

"I only talk to you," Plato said.

"That's not true. You told Clark that it was the lophos who bit me."

"I made an exception, but as a whole, I prefer to only talk to one person. Let's say it helps me conserve my energy."

"Yes, and you obviously need to do that, since you nap most of the day." Liv followed the noise, stepping over a pair of kittens wrestling in the kitchen. Something was simmering on the stove, a savory aroma wafting from the pot.

Rory was chopping wood in his pristine oversized backyard.

"Hey there," Liv said, gaining his attention. "I have news."

"John knows you're a magician," he said, setting his axe down.

"Damn it. Why is everyone stealing my reveal moment?"

"It's a conspiracy," Rory answered.

"How did you know?"

He shrugged, pulling a rag from his jeans to wipe his face. "I just knew."

"Oh, that's such bullshit."

Rory peeked at her from behind the rag as he wiped the sweat on his cheeks. He seemed to relax a bit. "Okay, fine. It was a lucky guess. But lies and secrets are like clothes people wear. When you free yourself of them, well, you look different."

Liv gazed down at her frayed jeans and t-shirt. "And I look different now?"

"You look less weighed down."

"I like that," Liv mused. "And it's true. I feel better knowing that he knows the truth and accepts me no matter what."

"Did you seriously doubt that he wouldn't?" Rory asked.

"Yes. There was a real possibility that he'd tell me I was crazy or to get out."

"Then you *are* crazy." Rory walked over to a work area

he had set up with burnt-out coals and a barrel of water and tools Liv didn't recognize. He retrieved a sheathed sword and carried it over to her.

Pulling the leather sheath off the sword, Rory revealed a short silver blade that caught the setting sun. The hilt was smooth, and Rory had inlaid blue gems. In the giant's hands, the sword appeared undersized, as if it had been made for a brownie. However, when he handed it to Liv, she realized it was the perfect size for her.

"Meet Bellator," Rory said, taking a step back as Liv wrapped her fingers around the hilt and froze for a moment. Her hand seemed to melt into it, becoming one with the weapon. Her eyes trailed to the fine point on its tip, taking in the expert detail.

"It's beautiful," Liv said in a hushed voice.

"We rarely describe a sword that way, but I'll allow it since the venom of the lophos is still making you talk funny."

Liv pursed her lips. "How *should* I describe it?"

"Well, it is a giant-made sword, which means that it will never dull or rust. For its whole life, the sword will look as it does today. And since it was made specifically for you, Bellator should lend you numerous benefits, but you'll have to train in order to learn what they are."

"'Bellator?'" Liv asked.

"Yes. The maker names each sword, and that's the one I've chosen for yours."

"What does it mean?"

"That you ask too many questions," Rory replied.

"Ha-ha," Liv said, moving the sword back and forth through the air, but not really knowing how to practice with it. "Are you going to teach me how to use Bellator?" When she was a child, she'd trained with her mother, but she didn't remember most of it. Actually, when she thought back, the memory of her mother and sparring with her only brought a tightness to her chest. She would have to get over that and remember what her mother taught her and improve upon it.

Rory picked up his axe and centered a log on the platform he was using for chopping. "No, I don't want to be a part of your combat training. I'll reserve my skills for training you how to use your spells and elemental magic."

"So that means you'll be teaching me how to throw fireballs?"

He swung the axe over his head, splitting the log cleanly. "The answer to that is still no. But I'll teach you other helpful things."

"Thanks, but who is going to teach me how to use the sword?" Liv asked.

Rory looked over his shoulder at her. "For that, you'll have to find a competent teacher. I suspect you know someone already if you're willing to let down your guard and trust them. However, I do have a warning."

Liv froze, waiting for him to continue.

"No one must ever know that I made this sword for you."

"Won't it be recognized as being giant-made, though?" Liv asked.

Rory swung the axe again, splitting another log. "It might, but you're not obligated to tell anyone where it came from or who made it."

"I don't understand," Liv said. "What's the harm in someone knowing that you made it?"

Rory turned around to face Liv, the axe resting on his shoulder. "The giants have not made a sword for a magician in a very long time. If anyone was to find out that the grandson of Rory Bemuth Laurens made a sword for a magician? Well, my days of peace would come to an end. Magicians can be unjust to giants, and elves and other races shun us from time to time. But no one is crueler to a giant than their own. Keep this between you and me, Liv."

"Of course. Always. And thank you. Bellator is..." Liv paused, searching for a better word than beautiful. A description that would make Rory know how much she appreciated the gift. "Bellator is magnificent."

Rory nodded, quiet pride taking up residence in his eyes. "You are welcome."

Liv tested the balance of the sword, swinging it through the air, noticing at once that her reflexes sped up. Her movements were cleaner, and strangely, her leg didn't hurt as she pivoted to slice through the air. Something had changed within her the moment she picked up the sword, and she looked forward to finding out how it enhanced her, as she knew it would. A sword made specifically for her by one of the greatest swordsmiths on Earth was bound to hold a special magic unlike any other.

Holding Bellator, Liv felt unstoppable. She felt like a Warrior who could take on the world.

SARAH'S AUTHOR NOTES

FEBRUARY 9, 2019

Thank you so much for reading and supporting the books. I'm so high on life after the release of the first book. Currently sitting in a hotel room in Las Vegas and pampering myself after finishing this book. Michael is out of town or otherwise I'd be pestering him to eat BBQ or nachos with me. BBQ nachos! Yum. Anyway, we didn't know how this series would be received, but the response has been amazing. Thank you again!

I've had a ton of fun writing this book. And you know who is extra happy about it? My daughter, Lydia. She told me the other day, "Mommy, I'm glad you're a writer because it ensures we always have something to talk about."

OMG, I freaking love that kid. And she's right. Being a writer does ensure I never had a dull moment and there's always weird shit going on in my head.

Speaking of Lydia, I modeled Sophia after her. She's smart, beautiful, beyond talented and fun. Also, a perk of being a writer's kid is that she got to name characters.

Sophia and Liv were both named by Lydia. Plato is modeled after my cat Finley. And Rory was inspired by a scientist friend of mine who is really a gentle giant. He may never know this though. Having a giant who secretly does nice things was a great Anderle idea. I planning for him to do other noble gestures which Liv will secretly find out about. I love people who do things because they are the right thing to do and not to get the praise or reward.

Every time I talked to Lydia about this book, she'd tell me that she was hungry for a cookie. It was always the mention of Brownies that got to her.

Okay, the maid is kicking me out of my room and I've got to get on the road. First though, BBQ nachos at The Henry. Love you all, lovely readers.

MICHAEL'S AUTHOR NOTES

FEBRUARY 10, 2019

THANK YOU for not only reading this story but these Author Notes as well.

(I think I've been good with always opening with "thank you." If not, I need to edit the other Author Notes!)

RANDOM (sometimes) THOUGHTS?

Donuts.

Ask me for anything around the Hotel Antlers in Colorado Springs, Colorado and I could probably get it.

Steak? The Famous Steakhouse is just two blocks away from the hotel.

Amazing food with a lot of Hatch chilis used in the recipes?

One block.

Heck, there was even a CHEAP Starbucks connected to the hotel. I know a Starbucks in a hotel is not that unusual. However, i'd probably spend at least twice as much money to purchase the same drink in a Starbucks in a hotel on the strip as I paid in Colorado Springs.

But, did they believe in donuts in that little area? No.

Certainly not donuts. If there was one, I didn't see it the few walkabouts I took to go to restaurants or the store to purchase gloves.

There is a saying that "nothing tastes as good as skinny feels."

Except donuts.

Donuts tell skinny it can go f*ck itself.

—-

THANK YOU for the awesome support this series has been receiving! I'm super jazzed you enjoy the merry band of characters we are sharing with you.

For most of my life, I thought my problem with stories was a mistake.

Something that should be contained, constrained, and caged up allowing me to focus on other projects.

Little did I know that instead of caging my thoughts, I needed to let them out.

AROUND THE WORLD IN 80 DAYS

One of the interesting (at least to me) aspects of my life is the ability to work from anywhere and at any time. In the future, I hope to re-read my own Author Notes and remember my life as a diary entry.

American Airlines flight coming back from Colorado Springs USA - Superstars Writing Conference (Kevin J. Anderson)

I'm in seat 2F sitting next to the window (dark outside, can't see anything.) I have two books worth of Author Notes I need to write and a book and a half of beats for a new project to finish by the time we make it to Las Vegas.

Hope I'm up to it. Right now my eyes are drooping.

Oh, and Metallica's Seek & Destroy just started playing in my headphones.

...

I'm ready to bang my head, but it is entirely inappropriate in first class. I'd ask my wife but the scathing glance she would give me would be sucky at best.

... That doesn't stop me from CRANKING IT UP!

FAN PRICING

$0.99 Saturdays (new LMBPN stuff) and $0.99 Wednesday (both LMBPN books and friends of LMBPN books.) Get great stuff from us and others at tantalizing prices.

Go ahead, I bet you can't read just one.

Sign up here: http://lmbpn.com/email/.

HOW TO MARKET FOR BOOKS YOU LOVE

Review them so others have your thoughts, and tell friends and the dogs of your enemies (because who wants to talk to enemies?)... Enough said ;-)

ACKNOWLEDGMENTS

SARAH NOFFKE

My favorite part of writing any book is creating the acknowledgements page. It reminds me that writing a book is not a solo task. I might sit alone and write, but the finished product is a result of the support and encouragement of a tribe of people.

Thank you to the readers who buy the books, read them, review and recommend. YOU are the one who keeps us writing. I'm always inspired by the messages I receive from readers. Thank you supporting the books and offering so much richness to my life.

Thank you to my LBMPN family for all the support. Steve, Michael, Lynne, Moonchild, Jennifer and so many others who help champion the book to publication and beyond.

Thank you to the beta readers who offered so many valuable insights early on. Thank you to John, Chrisa, Kelly, Martin and Larry.

Thank you to the JIT team for all the awesome feedback. A new series is always exciting and nerve-wracking.

Michael and I thought we had a great idea for a new world, but we don't really know until we get objective feedback. What would I do without all you awesome readers?

Thank you to my friends and family. Writing is a strange profession. I work weird hours, talk to myself, have a strange diet, get antsy about deadlines. But the wonderful people in my life continue to show their encouragement and thoughtfulness no matter what. It is never lost on me because I know that I wouldn't be doing what I love without all you amazing people, cheering me on.

And as with all my books, the final thank you goes to my muse, Lydia. I wrote my first book so that I could make my daughter proud, and it's never stopped. I write every book for you, my love.

BOOKS BY SARAH NOFFKE

Sarah Noffke, an Amazon Best Seller, writes YA and NA sci-fi fantasy, paranormal and urban fantasy. She is the author of the Lucidites, Reverians, Ren, Vagabond Circus, Olento Research, Soul Stone Mage, Ghost Squadron and Precious Galaxy series. Noffke holds a Masters of Management and teaches college business courses. Most of her students have no idea that she toils away her hours crafting fictional characters. Noffke's books are top rated and bestsellers on Kindle. Currently, she has thirty-three novels published. Her books are available in paperback, audio and in Spanish, Portuguese and Italian. http://www.sarahnoffke.com

Check out other work by this author here.

Ghost Squadron:

Formation #1:

Kill the bad guys. Save the Galaxy. All in a hard day's work.

After ten years of wandering the outer rim of the galaxy, Eddie Teach is a man without a purpose. He was one of the toughest pilots in the Federation, but now he's just a regular guy, getting into bar fights and making a difference wherever he can. It's not the same as flying a ship and saving colonies, but it'll have to do.

That is, until General Lance Reynolds tracks Eddie down and offers him a job. There are bad people out there, plotting terrible things, killing innocent people, and destroying entire colonies. **Someone has to stop them.**

Eddie, along with the genetically-enhanced combat pilot Julianna Fregin and her trusty E.I. named Pip, must recruit a diverse team of specialists, both human and alien. They'll need to master their new Q-Ship, one of the most powerful strike ships ever constructed. And finally, they'll have to stop a faceless enemy so powerful, it threatens to destroy the entire Federation.

All in a day's work, right?

Experience this exciting military sci-fi saga and the latest addition to the expanded Kurtherian Gambit Universe. If you're a fan of Mass Effect, Firefly, or Star Wars, you'll love this riveting new space opera.

NOTE: If cursing is a problem, then this might not be for you.

Check out the entire series <u>here.</u>

The Precious Galaxy Series:

Corruption #1

A new evil lurks in the darkness.

After an explosion, the crew of a battlecruiser mysteriously disappears.

Bailey and Lewis, complete strangers, find themselves suddenly onboard the damaged ship. Lewis hasn't worked a case in years, not since the final one broke his spirit and his bank account. The last thing Bailey remembers is preparing to take down a fugitive on Onyx Station.

Mysteries are harder to solve when there's no evidence left behind.

Bailey and Lewis don't know how they got onboard *Ricky Bobby* or why. However, they quickly learn that whatever was responsible for the explosion and disappearance of the crew is still on the ship.

Monsters are real and what this one can do changes everything.

The new team bands together to discover what happened and how to fight the monster lurking in the bottom of the battlecruiser.

Will they find the missing crew? Or will the monster end them all?

The Soul Stone Mage Series:

House of Enchanted #1:

The Kingdom of Virgo has lived in peace for thousands of years...until now.

The humans from Terran have always been real assholes to the witches of Virgo. Now a silent war is brewing, and the timing couldn't be worse. Princess Azure will soon be crowned queen of the Kingdom of Virgo.

In the Dark Forest a powerful potion-maker has been murdered.

Charmsgood was the only wizard who could stop a deadly virus plaguing Virgo. He also knew about the devastation the people from Terran had done to the forest.

Azure must protect her people. Mend the Dark Forest. Create alliances with savage beasts. No biggie, right?

But on coronation day everything changes. Princess Azure isn't who she thought she was and that's a big freaking problem.

Welcome to The Revelations of Oriceran. Check out the entire series here.

The Lucidites Series:

Awoken, #1:
Around the world humans are hallucinating after sleepless nights.

In a sterile, underground institute the forecasters keep reporting the same events.

And in the backwoods of Texas, a sixteen-year-old girl is about to be caught up in a fierce, ethereal battle.

Meet Roya Stark. She drowns every night in her dreams, spends her hours reading classic literature to avoid her family's ridicule, and is prone to premonitions—which are becoming more frequent. And now her dreams are filled with strangers offering to reveal what she has always wanted to know: Who is she? That's the question that haunts her, and she's about to find out. But will Roya live to regret learning the truth?

Stunned, #2

Revived, #3

The Reverians Series:

<u>*Defects*, #1</u>:
In the happy, clean community of Austin Valley, everything appears to be perfect. Seventeen-year-old Em Fuller, however, fears something is askew. Em is one of the new generation of Dream Travelers. For some reason, the gods have not seen fit to gift all of them with their expected special abilities. Em is a Defect—one of the unfortunate Dream Travelers not gifted with a psychic power. Desperate to do whatever it takes to earn her gift, she endures painful daily injections along with commands from her overbearing, loveless father. One of the few bright spots in her life is the return of a friend she had thought dead—but with his return comes the knowledge of a shocking, unforgivable truth. The society Em thought was protecting her has actually been betraying her, but she has no idea how to break away from its authority without hurting everyone she loves.
<u>*Rebels*, #2</u>
<u>*Warriors*, #3</u>

Vagabond Circus Series:

<u>*Suspended*, #1</u>:
When a stranger joins the cast of Vagabond Circus—a circus that is run by Dream Travelers and features real magic—mysterious events start happening. The once orderly grounds of the circus become riddled with hidden

threats. And the ringmaster realizes not only are his circus and its magic at risk, but also his very life.

Vagabond Circus caters to the skeptics. Without skeptics, it would close its doors. This is because Vagabond Circus runs for two reasons and only two reasons: first and foremost to provide the lost and lonely Dream Travelers a place to be illustrious. And secondly, to show the nonbelievers that there's still magic in the world. If they believe, then they care, and if they care, then they don't destroy. They stop the small abuse that day-by-day breaks down humanity's spirit. If Vagabond Circus makes one skeptic believe in magic, then they halt the cycle, just a little bit. They allow a little more love into this world. That's Dr. Dave Raydon's mission. And that's why this ringmaster recruits. That's why he directs. That's why he puts on a show that makes people question their beliefs. He wants the world to believe in magic once again.

Paralyzed, #2
Released, #3

Ren Series:

Ren: The Man Behind the Monster, #1:
Born with the power to control minds, hypnotize others, and read thoughts, Ren Lewis, is certain of one thing: God made a mistake. No one should be born with so much power. A monster awoke in him the same year he received his gifts. At ten years old. A prepubescent boy with the ability to control others might merely abuse his powers, but Ren allowed it to corrupt him. And since he can have and do anything he wants, Ren should be happy.

However, his journey teaches him that harboring so much power doesn't bring happiness, it steals it. Once this realization sets in, Ren makes up his mind to do the one thing that can bring his tortured soul some peace. He must kill the monster.

Note This book is NA and has strong language, violence and sexual references.

Ren: God's Little Monster, #2
Ren: The Monster Inside the Monster, #3
Ren: The Monster's Adventure, #3.5
Ren: The Monster's Death

Olento Research Series:

Alpha Wolf, #1:
Twelve men went missing.

Six months later they awake from drug-induced stupors to find themselves locked in a lab.

And on the night of a new moon, eleven of those men, possessed by new—and inhuman—powers, break out of their prison and race through the streets of Los Angeles until they disappear one by one into the night.

Olento Research wants its experiments back. Its CEO, Mika Lenna, will tear every city apart until he has his werewolves imprisoned once again. He didn't undertake a huge risk just to lose his would-be assassins.

However, the Lucidite Institute's main mission is to save the world from injustices. Now, it's Adelaide's job to find these mutated men and protect them and society, and fast. Already around the nation, wolflike men are being spotted. Attacks on innocent women are happening. And then, Adelaide realizes what her next step must be: She has to find the alpha wolf first. Only once she's located him can she stop whoever is behind this experiment to create wild beasts out of human beings.

CONNECT WITH THE AUTHORS

Connect with Sarah and sign up for her email list here:

http://www.sarahnoffke.com/connect/

You can catch her podcast, LA Chicks, here:

http://lachicks.libsyn.com/

Connect with Michael Anderle and sign up for his email list here:

Website: http://lmbpn.com

Email List: http://lmbpn.com/email/

Facebook:
www.facebook.com/TheKurtherianGambitBooks

49052039R00179

Made in the USA
Middletown, DE
17 June 2019